BRIDE

OF THE
SANTA FE TRAIL

BRIDE
OF THE
SANTA FE TRAIL

JEAN M. BURROUGHS

Sunstone Press
Santa Fe, New Mexico

FIRST EDITION
Printed in the United States of America

Library of Congress Cataloging in Publication Data:

Burroughs, Jean M., 1908-
    Bride of the Santa Fe Trail.

    1. Magoffin, Susan Shelby, 1827-1855—Fiction. 2. New Mexico—History—To 1848—Fiction.
3. Santa Fe Trail—Fiction. I. Title.
PS3552.U746B7   1984   813'.54   83-18051
ISBN: 0-86534-042-0

Published in 1984 by Sunstone Press / Post Office Box 2321 / Santa Fe, New Mexico 87504-2321 / USA

1

June 11, 1846:
Now the prairie life begins! Our mules travel well and we jogged on
at rapid pace. The hot sun or rather the wind which blew pretty
roughly compelled me to seek shelter in the shade of the carriage
and a thick veil.
So began Susan Shelby Magoffin's first diary entry. She was the
18-year-old bride of a husband 27 years her senior. She was his *querida*,
his companion on an adventure no American white woman had ever
attempted.

Privately tutored, accustomed to luxury, she was a paradox,
steeped in sheltered tradition but eager for the romance and hazards of
the Santa Fe trail. The blood of pioneers, soldiers and statesmen of
frontier Kentucky ran in her veins. Susan rode her thoroughbred mare
with the same skill she displayed in practicing with the hand gun she
packed in her trail *plunder basket.*

Samuel Magoffin, heavy-set and 45, had been a frontier merchant
with his brother James since 1828. Trading from Independence to Santa Fe to Chihuahua made him wealthy enough to offer his bride a
custom-made tent, a real bed with sheets, the black maid Jane and Indian carriage driver named Comapu.

On the first night of her memorable journey, Susan wrote:

– Our tent is a grand affair indeed, made in Philadelphia by a regular
tent-maker for the army. It is conical in shape, with an iron pole
and wooden ball (on top); we have a table in it that is fastened to the
pole and a little stand above it that serves for a dressing bureau. – It
holds our glass mirror and combs. Our bed is as good as many
houses have; sheets, blankets, a counterpane and pillows. We have
a carpet made of sail duck, portable stools, crossed with a pin
through the center – the seat part is made of carpeting.

Well, after a supper at my own table and in my own home – I
can say what few women in civilized life ever could, that the first
house of his own to which my husband took me after our marriage
was a tent; and the first table of my own at which I ever sat was a
cedar one, made with only one leg and that was a tent pole. But as I
said, after the first supper at my own table consisting of ham and

eggs, biscuit and a cup of shrub, I enjoyed a fine night's rest; it was
sweet indeed.

Next morning at daybreak Samuel woke her with a kiss. "Up, up, my love. The breakfast fires are smoking and the day is clear. We'll hit the trail by seven o'clock."

Susan snuggled against her pillow. "Seven o'clock! Detestable! I'm not used to getting up early."

"You're not in Kentucky, Susan, you're on the Santa Fe trail. Hurry."

"Come and get me then." Her face brightened with the provocative smile which first lured the staid bachelor who was now her husband.

With a wide sweep of his arm, he threw back the covers exposing Susan in her high-necked, long-sleeved, beribboned gown. The curves of her slender body were hardly unnoticeable. He scooped her up in a close embrace. What a marvel, he thought, that this high-spirited girl should be his wife.

She, too, marveled at the man who had only briefly courted her. Although Susan's older sister Anna had married Beriah Magoffin, Jr., her father had been most reluctant to approve the marriage. Their age difference and Samuel's dangerous life-style did not seem suitable for a Kentucky belle like his daughter and Susan's father was not easily won over by Samuel, but in the end his daughter's insistence prevailed.

"Oh, *mi alma,*" she said, "I'm so very happy to be here with you."

He put her down gently. "I'll send Jane to you with coffee while she helps you dress."

More asleep than awake, Susan sipped strong prairie brew made with coarsely ground coffee beans and creek water boiled hard in an enameled tin pot. Jane, who had tended her mistress since Susan was a child, chided her gently. "Hold your breath while I knot the strings of your corset, Missy." Then she added three layers of ruffled petticoats to fill out the full calico skirt of Susan's prairie dress. Lastly, Jane brushed Susan's thick dark hair into a loose bun, pinning her perky trail bonnet and heavy veil securely in place.

"You look just as good here as you did in Kentuck, Miss Susan. Now come get your breakfast 'cause Mister Samuel's waitin'."

Soon the camp echoed with cracking whips and violent cursing as impatient drivers beat the sluggish oxen into motion. Samuel smiled as Susan covered her ears to shut out the crude language.

"Why are the drivers so cruel to their animals?" she asked bitterly.

"Don't watch," answered trail-wise Samuel. "Those hides are thicker than you think. They'll soon pull without much whipping when they get used to the trail routine." Then he stood up in the carriage, flourished his own whip and shouted, "Stretch out, on the move, make time."

The wagon train began to creak its way across the prairie. Morning break-up of camp, nooning rest and repairs, pitching the Magoffin's tent at dusk, a routine repeated day after day. Susan was ashamed when she forgot which day was Sunday. Bouncing over rough terrain, circling mud holes, splashing through them, choking dust and searing heat blotted out the days of the week. But discomfort had little effect on her love of trail life.

> *June 15, Monday*
>
> *Tonight is my fifth en el campo. Oh, this is a life I would not exchange - such independence, so much uncontaminated air; I breathe free without uneasiness.*

One day Susan caught sight of a company of U.S. Dragoons sent to protect the traders.

"Look," she cried as the company passed the Magoffin wagons, "soldiers. We'll have no trouble reaching Bent's Fort ahead of schedule. There's nothing to fear now. Aren't you glad you brought me along?" she nestled against Samuel happily.

The following night their camp brought a different kind of delight to Susan. The creek in late June had begun to run a little lower so that large stones on the bed were exposed. Lifting her long skirts, Susan balanced from rock to rock, stepping back across the stream as if daring the rippling water to splash her trim ankles. Samuel smiled, always amused at her girlish enthusiasm. "Catch me a fish for supper," he cried tossing her a hook and line.

She swung the pole out toward a quieter pool near the exposed roots of an overhanging tree, trailing the line across the back water. However, in a few minutes, she complained, "Only a few minnows are nibbling my bait. You try your luck."

Then she jumped the stones, flung her arms about her head to stir the swarming mosquitoes.

Next night the whole camp was kept awake by the nerve-chilling howling of wolves. Ring, the greyhound that slept under Susan's side of the bed, growled deep in his throat at the prowlers and when the fires burned low and the wolves crept closer to the tent, Ring sprang up, barking fiercely. His sudden barks were as bloodcurdling to Susan as the howls of the wolves.

Listening to these hollow wails, Susan resented Samuel's peaceful snoring. Didn't he know she was frightened? Even Ring leaned over to lick her hand outside the covers before he went back to his accustomed spot. When the wolves finally slunk off, another wailing started up.

9

This time it was mosquitoes.

"Didn't you hear me slapping, slapping, slapping?" Susan demanded of Samuel rather crossly next morning. "I even hit your hand lying on the covers. Didn't you hear the wolves? Didn't you hear Ring? How could you sleep when I was so miserable?"

Samuel apologized. He knew there were worse hazards ahead requiring more stamina than Susan thought she possessed. "I'm sorry, Pet, tonight we'll rig up a netting over our bed. That will fend off the insects but I don't know about the wolves." Samuel soothed her with a fond stroking of her dark hair. He didn't mention the Indians who were more unpredictable than wolves or insects.

Noon of the next day, Jane brought a joint of freshly roasted meat to the tent for their meal. "Mr. Samuel wants you to slice off what you all need for your dinner. He asked me to go to the creek for more water."

"Oh, how good that smells," said Susan, bending over the savory roast. Outdoor life made her appetite keen and she found herself eating more than ever, even though Jane commented that her waistline was thickening. Susan began to slice with smooth, even strokes. The meat fell from the knife blade to amply fill Samuel's and her own tin plates.

Suddenly a shadow cut the bright prairie light streaming through the open tent flap. Then the doorway darkened. A huge, red-brown man, unclothed except for a breech clout, stared in amazement at the little white woman, the first he had ever seen.

Susan looked up, a scream of terror choked in her throat. The Indian's hand pulled a hunting knife from the belt of his breech clout. Susan's knuckled fingers whitened around the tent pole, her right hand clutching the heavy butcher knife. Eyes glazed from fright, she tried to speak out but found she couldn't.

The Indian looked at her for a long time then shifted his gaze to the meat. Susan lifted the large chunk and thrust it into his hand.

Where was Samuel? And Jane? Where had Ring gone?

The Indian holding the meat in one hand leaned forward with the other to touch Susan's soft cheek. Seeing no war paint rub off on his finger, he squatted on the tent floor and tore into the meat, greedily stuffing it into his mouth. The juices ran out of the corners of his mouth.

When Samuel arrived, the first thing he noticed was the Indian's headband – he was a member of the Kaw tribe – friendly Indians. Susan saw her husband was unafraid and slipped into a heap of calico skirts on the floor. Samuel shoved the Kaw toward the door.

"More grub, campfire, get more."

The brave moved without hesitation toward the campfire.

Samuel rushed to his wife, rubbing her hands, kissing her forehead and speaking in her ear. "Dearest, are you all right? Dear God, speak to me Susan, speak..."

She opened her eyes. "Oh, *mi alma*, he touched me! He rubbed my cheek. He had a knife!" She shuddered at the memory, sobs shook her slender shoulders.

"Be brave, dearest," Samuel said. "I must go and see where that Kaw went." Out the tent, he saw Jane coming up from the creek with a dripping bucket. Ring was beside her, wet and muddy.

"Go in to your mistress," he ordered shortly. "Don't leave the tent. Take Ring with you and tie up the flap. I'll send your meal by Jose."

In the meantime the hungry Indian had cleaned all the meat from the bone and was peacefully smoking his pipe beside the fire. He did not object when Samuel motioned for him to get up and pointed toward another wagon camp where a second bubbly pot could be shared.

Samuel dreaded the effect of this incident on his wife. He wondered if she would want to turn back at Bent's Fort. Susan surprised him, however, by sitting up in bed, recounting the terrifying experience to Jane. "Who at Arcadia would ever believe that my first real sight of an Indian would be *inside my own tent!* What would Papa think about the Indian fingering my cheek? Who would guess that he was more interested in food than scalp?"

"Good girl," Samuel said. "You offered him food instead of running. Your pioneer grandmother couldn't have been braver." Now he felt reassured. Susan had met her first danger with true courage.

The following noon, Susan watched for signs of crouching Indians in the wide vistas of waving grass.

"Samuel, look to the right! What's that brownish shape hidden in the grass? It's moving, coming toward us.!"

Something was indeed advancing toward their wagon. The parted grass swayed with movement. "The spy glass, look in the basket, hand it quickly," Samuel said. Fixing on the moving object, he watched a minute, laughed, handed the glass to Susan.

"Tell me what you see, Pet. What tribe does he belong to?"

"Why Samuel, it's a wolf, no, it's one of the camp dogs hunting. No, some animal I've never seen before. Here, look again and tell me."

"Susanita, that's a plains antelope. We'll see more I expect as they usually run in herds. I'll have to manage a nice roast for supper." He leveled his rifle at the creature. But the shot only hit the animal in the shoulder. "Well, there goes our supper," lamented Samuel as the then alarmed creature limped unevenly back through the grass.

"Oh, the pity of it," exclaimed Susan. "Now it will only suffer until the wolves find it, poor thing. At times life is harder for the beasts than it is for man. I'd rather go hungry than to have wounded it." Her eyes darkened with sadness.

2

Susan's mood of the afternoon lingered during the supper hour and her preparations for bed. Samuel noticed how she held her hair brush in mid-air while staring blankly into the tiny mirror.

"What's troubling you, Pet? Where's that happy smile?" he asked.

"Oh, I'm just remembering. We've been on the trail a whole week. Just think – we're more than a hundred miles from home! I'm wondering about those dangers we'll face, the things you warned me about before we left brother James' house in Missouri. You said I could stay there or even return to my family at Arcadia. Are you worried about how I'll meet our hardships? Are you sorry I came with you? Are you?"

He answered with a quick hug of assurance.

"Are *you* sorry? Do you want to go home?" His hands framed her face; eyes searched for an answer.

"No, no, *mi alma*, I want to stay with you – wherever on earth you may go. My place is with you."

"Then why are you so sad tonight?"

"I don't know. Maybe I feel you are keeping something from me."

Samuel was surprised by her intuitive reading of his own uncertainty. He pulled her down to sit close beside him on the bed. "It's best that you know, Susanita. You're right, I am worried, not about you, my dearest, but about brother Jim."

"Why, he's traveled this trail longer than you. He is probably almost up with us now."

Samuel shivered involuntarily, blew out the lamp flame, pulled the quilts snugly about them. "You remember that letter that Jim left me? It was on the dresser in our room."

"Yes, I asked you what he said."

"I'll confess, I didn't tell you everything then. He mentioned that there had been more military disputes with Mexico over the Texas border, and armed skirmishes at Palo Alto and Pesaca de la Palma on the mouth of the Rio Grande. I already knew that American fishing vessels had been seized by Mexican officials and that U.S. troops had entered their territory to protect settlers whose land rights had been questioned."

"What has that to do with Jim?"

"I'm not sure myself, but I feel something has happened. He should have joined us by now. You know how I hated to start this trip without kid-brother Will and Gabriel."

"Jim needed them to drive his wagons and guard his merchandise. They'll catch up with us," Susan said. Her fingers smoothed the wrinkles of his forehead, stroking his thin hair.

"What concerns me is why Jim had to go to Washington at all. Why did he need to see President Polk and Senator Benton? It most certainly has something to do with the state of war between the U.S. and Mexico but I just can't guess what Jim's part in it is."

"You knew about the war before we started. You knew troops would precede us to Bent's Fort. Samuel, we are safe, aren't we?"

"For the time being. But each day Jim doesn't join us, I worry a little more. I'm sorry, Pet. Let's go to sleep now – morning comes all too soon." He drew her close to him.

But Susan couldn't sleep, his embrace was too tight and this uncertainty about Jim along with her own nagging fears kept her wide awake. She tried to dismiss it but like Samuel she found she couldn't.

At dawn the dark blue clouds of night were etched with rose and mauve. Susan peeked out the tent flap. "How beautiful the prairie is," she exclaimed. "Kentucky was never created on such a scale of grandeur. I feel now like a child of the prairie, a true pioneer."

She turned to ask Samuel, "I wonder how soon other women will ride this trail? I'm the first, the very first – do you think history will remember that?"

Samuel smiled at this return to cheerfulness. "The very first, querida. You'll also be the first white woman to arrive at Council Grove by wagon train."

When they were on the trail again he told her how the thick cluster of hardwood trees had been named Council Grove when U.S. agents and Osage Indians met there in 1825; how the tribe agreed by treaty not to molest the men who were surveying a trade route from Independence to Santa Fe; how in later years Council Grove became a main stopping place on the trail west.

13

Captain Hall rode up on horseback, lifting his hat to Susan and asking her husband, "Shall we camp this side of the creek or cross over late this afternoon, sir?"

"Let's strike camp on that low hill farther down the trail. The creek there should run a deeper pool at its base."

Samuel turned to Susan with a grin, "Would you like to bathe in the Council Grove creek?"

Fighting seven days' dust, stirred by hundreds of hooves and iron rims of the heavy wagon wheels, Susan longed for cool water against her skin. "I can't think of anything nicer," she said with a sigh.

While the tent was being set up and the wagoners were unhitching the teams, Susan and Jane slipped off to a bend in the creek where dense undergrowth hid them from prying eyes. They didn't enter the water together but each took turns on guard while the other soaped and rinsed.

"It's absolutely the best bath I ever had," Susan said. Jane helped her into clean underclothes. She shook the dampness from her long hair and rubbed it vigorously with her towel. "Jane, did you ever before bathe right out in the open? In broad daylight?"

"Yas'm, I have. Us chilluns would splash around stark naked in the creek at Arcadia lots of times in the summer when our mammy was busy at your papa's house. I got my hide tanned good and proper onct when mammy thought I was too big a girl for such doins. Now hand me our dirty clothes and I'll scrub while you brush your hair dry."

A crackling of twigs underfoot and Ring's staccato bark made Jane duck for cover in quick alarm. The clear water of the creek scarcely obscured the outlines of her slender black body. She dared not come closer to the bank to catch the towel which Susan stood ready to throw her. Tall weeds on the opposite bank parted and a dark face framed in tightly curled black hair under a straw hat caught a glimpse of the two young women.

"Scuse me, ladies," stammered an embarrassed black man who scrambled up the muddy bank and disappeared.

"Jane, do you suppose he followed us here on purpose?" Susan said fearfully.

"I don't rightly know his name, but he's drivin' a team with Colonel Owens' train. I've noticed him before – hangin' round, tryin' to get friendly. I s'pose he just come down to wash hisself like we did."

Returning to camp, Susan recalled when she had seen the black man before. "Was he the one Colonel Owens' mule dragged around the camp the morning we left?"

"Yas'm, he's the one, but I don't recollect his name."

While fires burned to coals so that biscuits could be baked in

14

covered iron skillets, Susan hiked to the crest of the hill above their camp. She caught her breath. Miles and miles of grass, grass, grass – green in contrast to the red sky at sunset. This prairie doesn't heave and swell like the sea, she thought, it billows gently before the wind. Suddenly she felt an intense longing for home. Yet when she looked again at the endless prairie, unmarked by hill or tree, she was ready to accept almost any fate.

On the last night in camp, the group of 45 wagons were circled into a corral to keep the stock enclosed for quick departure next morning. Susan went to sleep with trail songs drifting on the air. The men sang all the verses of "Come all you bold teamsters."

Next day, instead of a bright sun promising good weather and easy travel, rain fell in torrents. There was great difficulty in yoking oxen, hard pulling through mud, the wagons stuck in the creek. The day was terrible for both men and animals. The only exciting thing, it seemed to Susan, was the unexpected arrival of Captain Charles Bent of Bent's Fort with about 20 horsemen on his hurried dash to St. Louis. While he and Samuel exchanged news of the trail and the worsening military situation in Mexico, Susan wrote a letter to her family which Bent promised to post in Independence.

She wrote nothing of the monotony of breaking and setting up camp, uncertain hours, tedious waiting in the carriage. She gave no hint of a strange feeling that had begun to plague her night and day, to unsettle her usual good health. No hint of questions she wanted to ask her mother. In her diary she wrote:

If I live through all this – and I think from all appearances I shall come off the winner – I shall be fit for one of the Oregon Pioneers.

Samuel leaned toward Captain Bent: "Will Governor Armijo close the trail to Santa Fe?" he asked. "What about fighting on the border?"

"I've just come from Santa Fe and, while I can't answer your questions for sure, I can tell you that the Governor is definitely alerted."

"We heard before we left Independence that Congress called for a limited war, " Samuel said. Then to protect Jim's mysterious mission he quickly added, "but it could be a camp rumor."

"No, it's true. I heard it confirmed at the Arkansas Crossing a few days ago. Armijo himself bragged to me that he might be reinforced by Mexican General Urrea and 3,000 to 5,000 men. Course it might be a bluff. He knew I'd pass along to authorities whatever scraps of information I had."

"Do you believe it to be a fact?" Samuel glanced toward the tent where Susan was writing.

"No way of knowing, none at all. I believe it's a brag, but I can't afford to ignore it. That's why I and my men took off in such haste – to warn the government.'' Bent looked grim.

When Susan appeared at the tent door, letter in hand, Samuel sloshed through the mud to get it. Then Bent spurred his horse and rejoined his men.

Samuel calculated the time since the last week of May when his brother Jim had started on the urgent journey to Washington. Now, a month later, when they themselves were only two weeks on the trail, he knew he couldn't reasonably expect Jim until sometime in July. How did he know that Jim would actually be able to contact him as promised? How could he be sure that his brother, in his great haste to reach Santa Fe, would not risk taking the dry route through the Cimarron cut-off? In that case, they wouldn't meet at all. His concern hardened into a small persistent frown.

Susan noticed his silence when they started on the trail toward the Arkansas River. The difficulty of traveling in steady rain added to everyone's hardship, and that night Susan could no longer overlook the streams of water that flowed across the tent floor.

"Here I sit in the middle of my bed like an island in the sea,'' she said to Jane. "Where's Samuel?''

"Right now your husband's talkin' to Colonel Owens. He says his camp looks like a pig wallow compared to you all's. He came to borrow some wood, but Mr. Samuel told him there isn't a smidgeon to spare.''

"I guess it's a cold supper again tonight,'' Susan said disparagingly.

"You don't *really* mind, do you?'' Samuel asked as he stuck his head through the tent flap. "Owens wants to speak to you before he goes back across the creek.''

"Evening, Miss Susan,'' greeted the tall man in western jacket and high, mud-caked boots. He removed his wide hat carefully and let the water drip down its brim to the muddy ground. "If all of us had as dry a nest as you have, there'd be none to complain,'' he commented, noticing Susan's writing desk, books and knitting bag heaped about her on the bed.

"Oh, I don't mind much,'' she replied. "Sometimes I spend rainy days at home doing what I'm doing now.'' Her smile seemed to make her visitor a little more cheerful himself.

"That's my Susan,'' chimed Samuel. "If there's anything good in a situation, she'll find it.'' His own tired face relaxed as he gazed fondly at her small figure, slender legs crossed beneath her calico skirt.

"Oh, messy as this is, I just call it one of the varieties of life I might as well accept, if not enjoy,'' she said.

Colonel Owens told them how one of his wagons was still stuck in the deep mud with the tongue broken beyond repair and with two wheels of another wagon in splinters. "If you need to pass me, you'll have to cut a path around. I may have to wait until the weather clears before I start again."

"I hate to leave you here, but we need to reach the Fort with all possible speed," Samuel said. "I'm hoping to meet my brother there and find out about the Washington trip. My other brother Will can catch up with you and help. He should be here soon."

An uncertain sun dawned next morning. Clouds, still dark with rain, hung gloomily overhead. And, by noon, sultry heat, without a breath of wind, made them as uncomfortable as the rain and damp clothing had the day before. When they undressed for bed Susan complained, "I'd like to sleep in my chemise instead of long gown. I'd even leave that off if I dared; it's so beastly hot."

"Why be so modest? Don't mind me!" Samuel grinned; he rolled up the sleeves of his long night shirt and left the high collar unbuttoned to his chest.

In the night gusts of wind visited the camp, driving off the heat. The tent canvas and metal fastenings of the center pole swayed in the blustery air. Lightning wracked the sky. Ring huddled on the extra quilt at the foot of the bed. Susan got up sleepily to push the heavy dog to the floor and a sharp pain in her side made her gasp. The pain spread across her abdomen, settling into a dull ache. While she lay awake searching her mind for a possible cause, she remembered some earlier strange sensations connected with this unexpected pain. Again she wished for her mother and rued the custom of the day that forced discussion of marriage and pregnancy to an embarrassed whisper.

At last she fell back into an uneasy slumber and woke to find Samuel already up and ready for the day. She decided not to bother him with her own puzzling uncertainties – at least not until she had to. She couldn't lower herself to ask her maid either, although she felt sure Jane would know. What a sorry state to be in, she thought, a victim of her fears in an unknown land.

The smell of coffee from the fires got her up for another day of riding, jolting, nooning, riding, jolting, jolting, jolting until dark.

"Here's your breakfast, Miss Susan." Jane placed a steaming cup of coffee and a plate of cold biscuits on the folding table. "Mr. Samuel said tell you he's short of wood again, the only fire in the whole camp is for the pot. He promised to stop early for dinner if he finds some wood. Ain't it queer to have no trees?"

"I miss the trees of home. Take the biscuits to Ring. I'm not hungry this morning." Susan pushed the plate away.

After Jane left, Susan sat on the side of the bed and tried to sip from the cup. Her hands trembled, her head swam and she was afraid of spilling the hot coffee all over her calico. She put the cup down, took up her knitting until Jose and Sandoval came to fold up the tent.

Samuel looked in with a fond smile on his face. He removed his hat and mopped his brow before leaning down to give Susan a kiss. "Since we're out of wood, we need to push on early to find another creek where the hands can gather dead wood from the banks. Otherwise there won't be any fires. The Bible teaches you can get your ox out of the ditch, even on Sunday, doesn't it?"

"Sunday, is this Sunday?" cried Susan in disbelief. "Oh, how I have been desecrating the Sabbath by knitting. How could I have forgotten?" She blushed to think of the stern lecture her father would have given her for such an infraction of religious rules at Arcadia.

"The Lord will forgive you this time," smiled her husband. "Now gather your things quickly and wait in the carriage."

She was slow to move. She didn't feel like riding. These last days, the Rockaway carriage had been jolting like a cart, bumping and swaying over the uneven trail.

The morning soon gave way to glaring sunlight which made Susan's eyes burn. She was glad for a temporary halt when the teamsters had to fill a swampy place in the road by packing tall grass in the muddy ruts. Afternoon wore endlessly on and the outriders kept reporting to Samuel that they hadn't located wood for fires or water for the animals. The emptiness of the prairie was upon them.

Wagons drawn by mule teams began to outdistance the oxen which could not withstand the heat and the ravages of thirst. When the exhausted creatures refused to pull, even under repeated lashings, Samuel rode ahead to confer with Captain Hall. "What do you make of it?" he called, mopping his brow, pushing the wet forelock from his reddened eyes.

"We'll have to stop before the animals plumb give out."

Susan didn't hear the rest of their conversation because one of the lead oxen fell in his tracks, splintering his yoke and snapping one of the chain fastenings. Her heart was moved to pity at the sight of the beast, and mild terror rose at the possibility of other animals dying.

She took out her diary to record the scene.

> One poor beast fell in the road. His driver, a tender hearted lad, went with a bucket to a mud hole, brought the cool mud to plaster over the animal's body. He gathered water from the kegs and poured it down the ox's throat. Then he covered it with blankets propped up by the ox yokes. I felt like crying."

Gradually the ox revived; a relief animal was hitched in its place.

Toward sunset the train continued to creak along the trail in search of water.

At last they approached a little ravine, Susan could see the loose stock break at the scent of water – such as it was. Samuel rode to the carriage to bring her a cup and also one to Comapu who had stopped singing only when his throat was too parched to croak out the words.

"Here, Susanita, sip it slowly," Samuel said, hoping she wouldn't see how much mud had been filtered out by the handkerchief stretched over the cup's rim.

"Thank you, dearest. I've never been so hot and thirsty. Still, I'm not as uncomfortable as you. Come rest in the carriage with me."

"Rest, you're asking me to rest? We've not found a camp site yet!"

"Couldn't we just stay here then?" she asked pitifully. "It's almost too dark to see."

"Susan, when it's fully dark, before the moon comes up, you'll be sorry you suggested this ravine. The mosquitoes would devour us. We can't possibly stay here just to suit you."

Susan had never heard Samuel be so cross with her. She leaned against the cushion away from him. The pain in her abdomen throbbed and a sudden realization of truth swept over her. Then a flood of tears she couldn't control. A baby born on this trail would not have much of a chance. But then the air was so thick with insects if she breathed at all, she feared she would suck them in. She fumbled in the darkness for her wicker basket, trying to find a veil for her face. The mules broke into a fast trot and the carriage swung recklessly from side to side.

"Jump, jump!" a voice commanded and Susan saw the dead oxen lying in the trail just as the mules crashed into it. Leaping from his horse, Samuel caught Susan in midair even before she jumped. Mules and carriage plowed heavily into the oxen.

It was past ten o'clock at night by the time the tent boys managed to set up quarters and stretch a net over Susan's head. She slept fitfully. Samuel fell in beside her, fully clothed, handkerchief knotted over his head, hands in pockets to protect himself from mosquitoes which clotted the air.

Next morning the July sun heaved up over the horizon with a furnace-like glow. A new month had begun. They were now 249 miles from Independence.

After every difficulty there seemed to be a few days' respite in which the whole group relaxed and regathered strength for the next test of endurance. Susan told Samuel: "Dearest, you've been so thoughtful of my comfort. Who ever traveled the Santa Fe trail in a Rockaway carriage and slept each night in a real bed? I feel like a spoiled child when I

19

think what others must have endured. I'm ashamed of myself."

"Susanita, I'm ashamed of myself, too. I look at your face and see dark circles under your eyes. Are you feeling ill? Maybe you'd better drink some wine and tonic."

She thought she should tell him what she knew of her condition but she was too tired for a long, perhaps tearful explanation. Later she slept soundly at Arrow Rock creek where the muffled ripple of water over ancient stones made for peaceful dreams.

The next few days travel was easier. They were approaching the flat land of the west. The first herd of buffalo were sighted grazing near the trail; prairie dogs in great numbers popped from their holes only to dart back before the camp dogs rushed them underground.

At sunset the wagons of Colonel Owens halted to dig a grave for a Mexican hand who had died during the day. Wrapped in his saddle blanket, wearing boots, wide straw hat placed over his face as protection from clods of dirt, his body was lowered down. Stones weighted the corpse to prevent its being dug up by marauding wolves.

The Magoffin caravan passed by as the grave was being filled in, grassy sod replaced, a cross of sticks stuck in at his head. Susan turned to her Bible and read aloud: "The Lord giveth, the Lord taketh away, blessed be the name of the Lord." She breathed her own prayer for the departed soul.

Their camp that night on the bank of the Arkansas River was quiet and subdued. Familiar songs around the fire had a comforting sound. Deep masculine voices boomed out the words of the Old Hundreth psalm: "All people that on earth do dwell." Over the still land the harmony lifted and swelled then faded before another singer began "A Mighty Fortress Is Our God." She thought, sleepily, that's Martin Luther's hynm. He was a pioneer too, but in a different way. She thought of home, but home was 300 miles and three weeks away. She turned her thoughts toward the end of the journey and Santa Fe, wondering if there would be another death, wondering whose it would be.

3

"How are we going to celebrate the 4th of July today?" Susan asked.

Samuel looked at her and laughed. "Celebrate the 4th? What with? We can't waste ammunition just to make a big noise."

"Oh, *mi alma*, you're so practical. Can't you think of something special once in a while? I have a surprise for you, and I want the day to be very special for both of us – a time we will always remember." Susan drew down her mouth with a sigh of disappointment. Her dark eyes clouded and lost their sparkle.

Her husband, usually eager to grant her requests, looked at her in a thoughtful manner. After all, she was a girl, still full of zest and love of social events. He had to admit to himself that there had been very little diversion for her since they started. "I'll try to think of some way for you to observe the 4th and surprise me too, if that would make you happy," he said.

At his tentative promise Susan brightened considerably. "Where are we headed today? Maybe we'll find a place along the trail." She had privately recovered from the shock of her pregnancy and, in fairness in her husband, she wanted to tell him, in a special way, a special place. Are all young brides so full of romantic notions she wondered.

"I tell you what, Susanita, when we reach Pawnee Rock, we'll stop for you to carve your name and date, maybe even climb to the top for a look at the scenery."

"That's as good a celebration as I could want and I'll thank you for stopping," she exclaimed. Her happy expression soon changed to a frown of alarm. "Why is it called Pawnee Rock? Are Indians lurking about there?"

"Not often," Samuel replied.

Susan's eyes glowed at what she heard. What better location could she ask to reveal her secret than this historic place?

When they reached the high redstone escarpment at noon, Susan, Samuel and Jane clambered the rocky face. On a ledge that provided good footing and a view of the heights above as well as the path below, Susan paused. "Let me have your hunting knife so I can scratch my name while you stand guard."

"Come now, Susan," her husband said as he watched her carve, "don't you remember that the dragoons recently came this way? They would have warned us of danger before now."

She finished the last letter with a little flourish, handed the knife for Samuel to add his name. "Jane, go back and tell Captain Hall we'll be along in a minute."

Samuel carved only S. Magoffin before sheathing his knife. He turned to take her hand and help her to a spot which, for thousands of years, must have been a lookout point for countless natives as well as the hunters and traders who followed.

She stood a moment in enchanted silence. "Oh, oh," she exclaimed at the unbelievable sight. "I didn't know how limitless the plains could be. There are no bounds –" she paused and her voice sank to a whisper, "just like my love for you, there are no bounds –"

Samuel's fingers tightened around her hand.

"– just like my love for the child that will soon be ours." The words tumbled out, not exactly as she had planned, but there could be no doubt as to her meaning.

"My dearest, is it true?" Samuel's voice quavered. "Are you sure?"

"Yes, and sooner than I realized –. But when we become parents, we'll be in Santa Fe for the winter in a snug little house all our own. You can tend to your trade and I'll tend our baby."

His arms enclosed her in an ardent embrace. They clung together on the rock pinnacle, pitting their deep love for each other against the unknown adversity of their life on the trail.

At Ash Creek they found that all but two of the wagons had already crossed over, there being no flowing water or rocky banks to hinder them. Comapu gaily sang in time to the rapid pace of the team.

"Lupita, tu eres hermosa, Lupita you are beautiful
Como los rayos del sol, Like the rays of the sun."
He did not slow down as he usually did when approaching a crossing, but continued his song in time to the hoof beats of the mules.

"Whoa," shouted Samuel to the team. "Whoa, whoa."

Comapu didn't miss a word of his song. Perhaps he didn't hear. The mules trotted faster and faster.

"Whoa, whoa," screamed Samuel again. It had always been his personal rule to walk, not ride down an embankment. Then seeing it was too late to jump out, he shouted, *"Adelante!* Go ahead, Go ahead."

The carriage careened dangerously at an angle down the slope, Comapu at last pulling on the reins, shouting Spanish at the run-away mules. The carriage inverted itself in a complete flip. Samuel threw his body protectively over Susan but fell heavily upon his left arm and hip in his attempt to shield her. Luggage, guns, baskets, metal boxes, bottles flew out of their stowaway positions and scattered amid parts of the carriage. Susan lay unconscious, fallen half way over the step, her limp arms hanging below her head as if she were dead.

The weight of the overturned carriage stopped the wild team. Comapu leaned over to help his master to his feet. *"Lo siento, lo siento,* I'm sorry," he repeated over and over. He helped lift the debris from Susan's body so that Samuel could gather her in his arms and place her gently on the ground.

"Licor, licor," shouted Samuel urgently, *"botella de licor."* He saturated his handkerchief with potent brandy, holding it under her nose and wiping her face and hands with it in a frantic effort to revive her. "Susanita, oh my Susanita, what have I done to you, to our little one. Forgive, forgive." He buried his face in her hair as he continued to massage her hands.

Soon her eyelids began to flutter and her breathing became deeper. "What happened? Why am I on the ground? Is that *liquor* I smell?"

"Shhh-hhh rest quietly, dear, until I can get the Dearborn. Then we'll place you in Jane's nice bed."

They traveled so slowly the rest of the afternoon that it was quite late in the evening when they caught up with the wagons. Government orders had stopped the train at Pawnee Fork until the arrival of extra troops. How glad Susan was for this delay! How grateful Samuel that his brave wife was only momentarily stunned.

At least 150 wagons had assembled at the Fork on the Arkansas River. What a sight the camp made with great circles of white canvas in corral formation, greyed over with smoke from cooking fires that spiraled into the reddening sky. Military uniforms of dark blue wool with brass buttons stood out next to the brown drabness of plainsmen's clothing. Jovial shouts, raucous laughter, marching songs mixed with the rhythmic strum of guitars. It was a noisy, gay company, resting from the rigors of long travel. When news of Susan's accident spread through the camp, she became the center of attention. Young Army officers stopped by her tent to pay respects. She basked in the glow of their gallantry, smiling coquetishly at them as if she were still an unmarried Kentucky belle.

For the next week traders and soldiers engaged in hunting, drying buffalo jerky and feasting on the tender, delicious hump meat. Susan wrote her father of the great herds which came within gun shot of the camp. "It's better than venison, Papa, I wish you could taste this meat."

Samuel was not so content, however. He chafed under the delay, worrying that James might miss him along the trail somehow, fretting of the outcome of the Washington conference. At this time the danger was not from Indians as much as from Mexican forces ranging north from Santa Fe to attack American wagons entering their territory. Finally permission arrived by outrider from Colonel Stephen Watts Kearny, Commander of the Army of the West, that the caravans could proceed as far as Bent's Fort on the Arkansas River.

The Magoffin wagons got underway next morning, a day of heat and burning dryness. Susan's shake-up began to have a delayed effect.

July 11, Saturday
> Oh, how gloomy the plains have been to me today. I am sick,
> have rather sad feelings and everything around corresponds to them.

All her effort to conceal the fact could not deceive the solicitous Samuel. He noticed her unusual quietness. It was Sunday. Her Bible lay in her lap but she didn't read it. Once when she felt his glance upon her she said, "I was just thinking that the ringing of church bells and attendance at public worship isn't necessary for prayer. I was giving thanks for many blessings."

"And I give thanks, dearest, that you weren't seriously injured. I still fear for our little one. Oh, God, would that it had not happened."

The next day, the next and the next, each in turn, saw her grow more shadowy and weak. Samuel sent ahead for a doctor whom he knew to be in the army train preceding them. The physician agreed to wait until Susan could be driven forward to receive his attention. Oh, what a relief Samuel felt in turning the ailing Susan over to him. Even an Army doctor used to treating men's wounds and broken bones would have had some training in women's illnesses, he thought.

"A birth is a very normal function, madam," the doctor stated in stiff professional manner after he had checked her. A trim Frenchman, Phillipe Auguste Masure, M.D., he bowed low over her pale little hand in an exaggerated gesture of courtliness. He was a product of the old school of medicine where doctors attended even the most difficult cases in formal attire of waist coat and tails. His hair curled low over his collar and his neatly trimmed and waxed moustache bristled to a point.

The very sight of him filled Susan with encouragement. "Do you really think I'll be all right, doctor? Do you think any harm will result to my -" she broke off, blushing furiously. To discuss such subjects with a man, even before she told her mother, despite the fact he was a doctor, seemed indecent.

"My dear young lady, haven't you always enjoyed good health?"

"Oh, yes indeed. I was never sick at all except when my sisters passed on the measles when we were children."

"Then that's in your favor now," he assured her. "Before you sleep tonight, take two of these tablets to relax. All you need is quiet and rest."

Susan watched him repack his black bag with its vials and pill boxes. She sighed gratefully that there had been no dire prediction. However, inwardly she was terrified, fearful of the dreadful distance separating her from home and the loving care she would have received there; fearful, not of pain to herself, but of possible injury to the unborn life within and, lastly, fearful that now she would be a hindrance to her husband when he needed her most.

Samuel accompanied Dr. Masure back to the army wagon. "is there anything, anything at all I can do for her?" His anxiety puckered his brows while he nervously ran his handkerchief over his sweaty face and neck. "Oh, I blame myself for all of this. I should have kept a closer check on our driver. She had just told me of the expected child. I was so overjoyed –"

"Listen," the doctor said in a fatherly voice, although Samuel was practically the same age, "you need to keep cheerful and boost your wife's spirits all you can. Anxiety is the worst possible emotional strain for her just now."

"But sir, will there be a dire outcome?" asked Samuel.

"That I cannot tell, only time and her natural stamina will determine. Do keep in touch with me. I'll arrive at the Fort before you do." As Samuel turned to leave, Dr. Masure laid a hand on his arm. "I understand your concern. She's so young, so delicate in form, like a little prairie rose. May I ask you why she agreed to make such a journey?"

Samuel was surprised but he answered truthfully. "It was her desire to be the first American woman on the trail. I could not dissuade her."

"Good," answered the doctor. "She has will power. It may pull her through this ordeal." He raised his hand in a good-bye salute and Samuel turned his horse to ride back to the Dearborn.

Like a guardian angel Jane tended her mistress. "Nothin' goin' to happen to you, Miss Susan, if I can help it. I'm fixin' to watch you like I did when you was a baby."

"Jane, you're kind to me, so patient. I hate to be riding in your bed, but Samuel says the men are working to repair the carriage at every stop. I hope it won't be long."

"That don't worry me, so long as you're comfortable."

Jane could perform all the duties of a good nurse but she couldn't control the weather. That night a thunderstorm of incredible intensity disturbed their camp shortly after the tent had been pitched and Susan put to bed. Rain, wind, thunder, lightning assailed the fragile shelter, beat upon the canvas tops of the wagons. No human voice could be heard above the violent rumbling and clashing. Samuel shouted for the tent boys but no one came.

In the darkness he helped Susan pull on a dress over her nightgown while he stuffed his nightshirt into his riding breeches and crammed his feet into heavy boots. "Hold the tent pole," he shouted, though the wind howled his words away before she could obey. Instead she grasped the foot of their bed.

And that was what saved her from further injury. When the tent collapsed, she fell onto the mattress, shaken and defeated but still unharmed. Samuel couldn't reach her. The folds of canvas engulfed him. "Dear God," he cried in distress, "save us."

Groping in the black on hands and knees, he found the bed and Susan. Together, they made their way to the Dearborn, calling through sheets of falling rain for Jane to unbutton the curtains. "Wrap her up warm," Samuel shouted. "She's drenched through and through." He turned to find the tent boys were searching in the tumbled canvas for their master and mistress. He helped them tie the wheels of the light carriage to a baggage wagon, lest the force of the wind push it over like a child's toy.

"I pray the good Lord that nothin' more happens to you, Miss Susan. I'm plumb give out with worryin' and prayin'," Jane said as she tucked layers of blankets over Susan, then lay down close beside her to share the warmth of her body.

"I've had my share of trouble, Jane," she whispered wearily and, though she closed her eyes, there was no sleep for either of them that turbulent night. Susan kept hearing in her mind the howl of wolves from that other night when a prophesy of doom seemed to seal this ill-fated expedition.

Fortunately the following days passed uneventfully: thunder, Indian sign, a few bad creek crossings. Once Susan found a sword and bunch of sticks on the side of the trail. "What is the meaning of that?" she asked Samuel.

"It was a warning to any tribe that the U.S. Army was also on the trail; the great pile of sticks indicates many soldiers in the company."

"Do you suppose Indians have seen the troops that are traveling ahead of us?"

"Of course. Scouts are out all the time, relaying news to their chief by smoke signals, sounds, bent twigs, anything that will show soldiers on the march."

Susan was relieved to hear this and especially glad when Captain Moore came to their tent to inquire. "I trust you're recovered from your fall, madam. All of the troops wish you the best of health."

The sight of the young captain from Kentucky was like a tonic. Other soldiers crowded around for the sight of a woman, especially a pretty one, and the chance for some conversation. They feasted their eyes upon her, longing for their wives back home. Susan blushed under their stares and tried to fasten the last buttons of her bodice over her expanding waistline.

Her eyes sparkled, however, in spite of embarrassment and her bright smile lighted her face which was becoming pinched and drawn under the constant difficulties of travel. Samuel watched indulgently, hoping that the soldiers' presence and the security of Bent's Fort would be beneficial to her condition.

Upon arrival at the castle-like Fort the next day, Samuel felt an immediate urgency to get Susan safely inside the walls. They passed the sentry and approached the huge mud palace, built like an ancient fortress with two high look-out towers at opposite corners.

"How many times have you visited this place before?" Susan asked, gazing in wonder at the immensity of adobe walls.

"Many, many times, but it looks better to me now than ever before." He directed Comapu to drive to the tunnel-like main entry, high and wide enough to allow the largest of freight wagons to pass through. They paused before the massive gate, its planking reinforced with iron, and waited for the guard's appearance at one of the high slits in the wall.

"Who goes there?" questioned a rough voice. Susan caught a glimpse of a gun barrel pointing straight at their carriage.

"Samuel Magoffin, trader, Independence, Missouri, and my wife who is ill."

"We're full up. Can't take any more inside the walls. Sick soldiers have filled all our space," the guard said.

"I'm a friend of the Bents. My brother James Magoffin is well acquainted. We must have shelter; my wife is expecting a child."

Susan blushed at the declaration of her condition, but modesty was cast aside in the urgency of the moment. She heard a low command from inside the tower.

Samuel glowered impatiently, his lips compressed to a thin line. "Lean against the cushion; look sicker than you are," he whispered.

Susan didn't feel deceitful in closing her eyes with a weary sigh. At the thought of being turned away from safety, tears trickled down her pale cheeks.

In a moment another face appeared at the narrow window slit. It was William Bent himself and he recognized Samuel and gave the order to admit them. "Sorry we're so crowded," he explained as they came through. "Ever since the army came, it's been pure hell. One demand after another – All I can give you is a bare room, not even a chair, but there's an old mattress on the floor."

"We have our own furniture which we've used in our tent," Samuel said. "If you show us where to put it, we'll unload immediately. My wife must lie down."

Upon Bent's order, their baggage wagon rolled into the plaza. Samuel directed the carrying of their furniture by sweating tent boys up an outside stairway to a second floor room. One narrow window opened upon the plaza and the opposite one offered a view of the wide barren plain where more soldiers were encamped. Soon a messenger came to announce that Colonel Kearny had already arrived.

Susan was led by an Indian woman to wait in the *sala* or large parlor, a room where seats were rolled-up blankets along two sides of the adobe wall. Here the belle of Kentucky took her place with the wives of the Bent brothers and of a trader named Leitensdorfer from Santa Fe. She sank gratefully to the cushion with a brief nod to the other women. *Buenas dias* was all she could think of to say. There were three races sitting about the room and Spanish, Anglo, Indian soldiers and traders milled back and forth. Many of them came for water which was drunk from a common dipper, the unused portion dashed to the earthen floor to settle the dust. Susan cringed when more than once some of the splash landed on her skirt. She tried not to show surprise at any crude actions, but they stared at her, beginning with her little bonnet with veil pinned back, the fine quality of her dress and, above all, her high-top, laced shoes. The other women wore mocassins.

However, she was as curious as they were, staring in amazement when one of the Indian women loosened her long, black hair, combing, greasing and letting it hang loosely over her shoulders as if preparing for bed. Susan wondered if any of the other women would do the same.

Then Samuel came to escort her to their room where Jane was working to make things presentable. Samuel insisted she sleep on the mattress placed outside their door in case she was needed during the night.

"This isn't bad at all," Susan said when she saw her own familiar chair, table and bed installed in the tiny room. "At least it doesn't have a tent pole to collapse, or canvas to flail in the wind and rain."

"How we gonna fix our food, suh?" Jane asked.

"It will be prepared by the wagon cooks and brought to us. We'll eat right here," he answered. "In fact, we'll stay until I have a chance to talk to my brother."

Susan was glad to hear him say that. She wanted nothing more than to stay and rest. "Are all these people here because of the war, because of an Indian scare?"

"No, this is unusual because of the Army being quartered here, but the Bents maintain a self-sufficient trading operation and it takes many helpers to handle it. When you're rested, we'll walk downstairs to see the dining room, kitchen and store."

She dismissed Jane to write to her family while Samuel sought his brother whom he had heard had just arrived.

Dr. Masure was in the group of wagons and upon Samuel's request he paid a call on Susan, bringing medicine and calming advice. "Next time you want to go traveling, young lady, have your husband take you to Europe instead of across a wild country like this."

Susan laughed, "Oh, Doctor, I've had quite enough traveling of any kind." Then she added wistfully, "I thought this trip would be good for me. I wanted to have things happen; to be different from my sisters, to have each day bring new adventures. Samuel warned me it would be hard, but I didn't know *how* hard –"

"You're a plucky young woman. Follow my instructions and don't exert yourself in any way. Tell your husband to send for me whenever you need assistance."

The next day was July 30th, Susan's 19th birthday. She was cheered by visits from the same group of attentive officers who had greeted her earlier. With wine from the Magoffin wagons they drank toasts to her, holding tin cups aloft, touching them together as they saluted her. "To your good health, madam," and "Our compliments on your birthday, Mrs. Magoffin." Samuel beamed at their attention as it seemed to make Susan happy. Captain Johnson sang in a high clear tenor the new popular Irish lovesong, "Believe Me If All Those Endearing Young Charms" which everyone thought quite appropriate. The officer directed his ardent gaze at Susan until she blushed in confusion.

Samuel then became serious and asked Captain Moore about the state of affairs while the officers regaled Susan with stories of their trail experiences. Though she was talking vivaciously, her huband noticed that she pressed her temples and passed a hand over her eyes in a tired gesture. "I think it's time we all took our leave," he said firmly to Susan. "You rest while we go outside to the camp ground."

Samuel then sought out his brother James. The suspense of not knowing about James' secret government mission, along with his concern for Susan was beginning to make deep lines above his brow. "Let's ride out on the prairie," he said after he found and greeted his brother. "We can talk and not be overheard."

When they were some distance from camp, James spoke: "The President's mission is rather simple. He calls it 'manifest destiny.' Something about the nation's right to possess the North American continent as God-given. Sounds simple, but it could be disastrous to me personally. The mission for which I have been chosen at Senator Benton's suggestion, though God knows why, is to go ahead of Colonel Kearny's forces and soften up Governor Armijo in Santa Fe. I am instructed to make certain offers to persuade him of the advantages of a peaceful *entrada* by the Army of the West. We don't believe the Mexicans' brag that thousands of men defend their capitol. We think, at least we desperately hope, that Armijo will listen while he enjoys the finest of our wines.''

"Do you have an official document to show him?" questioned Samuel. He knew Jim's special kind of blarney was persuasive, but he also knew that such a proposition was only official when put in writing.

"Of course, I have a letter from the Secretary of War to explain the President's plan to Kearny. He, in turn, has already presented Captain Cooke with a letter to the governor. This should convince Armijo that troops are being sent only to keep peace and give protection. In addition, the Secretary of War has sent copies of his proclamation to Taos. I'm to tell Armijo that I've been dispatched by President Polk, and that establishing peace is the only mission of the Army. However, the government plans to take possession of all New Mexico land east of the Rio Grande River as a part of the territory annexed to the United States when Texas joined the Union."

"Do we have any right to land-grab like that?" Samuel asked in disbelief.

"That's my purpose, I guess, to convince him that we do have a right, backed by the Army. I'm to persuade him that to honor our claim peacefully would be within his best interests. If he listens to my advice it will be because he is a cousin to my former wife, Maria Gertrudes."

"May the Good Lord rest Maria's soul and be with you as well, Jim," Samuel said as he leaned from the saddle and shook hands with his brother. "Now I must get back to check on Susan. Coming with me?"

Samuel was glad Susan was asleep when he entered their room and quietly undressed. But for a long time he lay awake thinking how his brother might be seized and thrown into prison in Santa Fe. Kearny had only a limited number of soldiers with him and Samuel dreaded the consequences of a possible fight.

Even had his thoughts been at ease, Samuel wouldn't have slept well that night for Susan was restless, moaning in her sleep, crying out in pain. As soon as it was light enough to see, he roused Jane from her pallet to stay beside her mistress. "I'm going to find the doctor," he told her. "I think the accident in the carriage is taking its toll."

But Dr. Masure was trying to save soldiers who had raging fevers in one of the rooms downstairs. One man had died during the night, two others lay in a coma. He sent word he would attend Susan as soon as he could get away. Samuel sat by her bed, bathing her burning forehead with water chilled by winter ice stored in the Fort cellar. Her eyes were glazed with pain. All day he waited, watching the door with a fixed stare. Toward evening the exhausted physician entered the darkened room, sank heavily into a chair. After the examination, Samuel asked, "Doctor, can you save –?" He couldn't bring himself to finish.

"I don't think there's much danger to the mother, but she will probably lose the fetus. In view of your present situation, Magoffin, I'd call that a blessing."

"Can't you give her something to relieve the agony?"

"Only later. I'll get morphine to tide her through the worst. I have a little left from my last amputation, but I must use it very sparingly." At dawn it was over and Susan sank into a deep sleep, cradled in Samuel's arms. When Jane came to relieve him, he said, "Don't leave, under any circumstances, until I return."

The woman watched while he picked up the blanketed remains from the foot of the bed. "Tell her, if she rouses, that I've gone to prepare for a Christian burial. I know she would want that."

Sometime during the morning Susan woke to hear the lusty cries of a newborn infant. "Is that my baby?"

Jane answered slowly, "That baby belongs to an Indian woman downstairs. I watched her take it to the river and bathe it right after I heard its first cry."

The words trembled on Susan's lips, "And mine –?"

Jane watched from the window as Samuel dug the tiny grave in the corner of the plaza.

At intervals during the next day Susan was roused from sleep by the sounds of military departure. Blacksmith hammers, trumpet blasts, thumping of hooves, clinking of swords, the ominous tolling of the Fort bell through troubled dreams. She tried to rise but Jane, still sitting beside her, comforted her back to sleep. Sometime after, a loud summons on an army bugle made her sit up straight. "What is that noise? It makes my ears throb. My head aches, oh, it aches."

"The soldiers are starting for Santa Fe. Least ways that's the camp rumor," Jane said.

"Without us? Without the Magoffin wagons? Where is Samuel? He wouldn't leave us here, would he?" Susan got up from her pillow and sank back with a faint moan.

Samuel came and went quietly, trying not to disturb her. Once she roused to see him standing by the bed, she raised a cold hand, showing blue tracery of veins. "Stay with me, Samuel, I'm so lonely."

"*Mi querida*, James is ready to leave with Captain Cooke. I need his final instructions concerning the disposition of his wagons if –" He paused, thinking further explanation of James' increasing danger would upset her. "His situation is uncertain now."

"*I* need you as much as *James*," Susan said crossly.

"I know, dear, I know, but the entire responsibility for our monetary investments rests with me until Will and Gabriel Valdez catch up with us. God knows when that will be. I have to stay near the wagons. Captain Hall can't oversee everything. Idleness makes for trouble in a trail camp like this. There have already been boisterous arguments among the men over grazing spots and water. In this summer heat both are becoming scarce."

"Do you think I ought to risk that carriage just yet? You know the doctor said –"

"My dear, I don't want to risk anything. Would you consider staying here with Jane and the driver until I can follow the wagons to Santa Fe and return to take you home?"

"In this dreadful place? Oh, how could you suggest such a thing? I'm stronger than you think." She started up from bed, fell back dizzily, sobs shaking her slender shoulders, her dark hair covering her tears.

Samuel set her down on the pillow. In his heart he knew he couldn't leave with the troops and the traders. He knew that to stay and make the trip later with small groups of wagons and baggage would make an ideal target for both Indians and Mexican troops. Hadn't he seen a warrior, believed to be a spy, in the plaza last night? Hadn't three Mexican spies been caught and searched? But looking down at Susan, he had no choice. He would have to wait.

He tiptoed from the room and started down the outside stairway. What a sight met his eyes! The Army of the West on the move! A stiff gale from the high Sangre de Cristo range ruffled his hair and made him shiver. Or was it apprehension? The wind's westerly direction stretched out the army banners and smaller guidons, pointing them straight east – toward home and safety. But the army was headed south into Mexican territory. Dust from hooves and wheels rose in the prairie wind. Samuel could see the vanguard moving out smartly with Colonel Kearny in the lead. Had James and the advance party gone without a final word to him? Had it happened while he was with Susan? There were endless questions with no answers.

He hurried down the stairs, his attention caught by shouts and salutes from a vast crowd above him on the parapet. The people in the Fort were cheering. "*Viva, viva el ejercito!* Long live the army," shouted the Americans. Low guttural tones rose from Indian throats. It was a dramatic and stirring sight, but Samuel couldn't stay to watch. He couldn't believe that James had left without contacting him. He made haste toward the *sala* where he heard laughter and tinkling glasses. Who would be drinking so early in the morning? Samuel guessed it would be nobody but the convivial James.

He entered the main room at the instant his brother toasted, "To the army, to Colonel Kearny, to Captain Cooke!" Scouts and dragoons in the advance party raised their own glasses to join him in the toast.

It was desperate gaiety, a last gesture of confidence before facing a common danger. Samuel was alarmed to see that the advance parties had not left before the army, according to plan. He caught James' eye and motioned for him to join him in the corridor.

"Why the delay? Is your mission called off?"

Jim threw an arm over his brother's shoulder. "Don't worry, fellow, we'll catch up with them and forge ahead before nightfall. No use waiting in that wind. It will be a long dry stretch; come join us in a drink. You look like you need one."

"Jim, you haven't told me what you want done if things don't turn out well for you." Samuel cleared this throat uncertainly. He looked down at his dusty boots. "There's no use denying –"

At this point Captain Cooke approached with a glass for Samuel and the opportunity for a confidential chat with James was lost. After a last toast he followed the men through the tunnel-like entry. The massive gates opened, clanged behind them.

It was August 2, 1846.

Samuel drew a deep breath as he watched his brother climb into a carriage beside a huge man called Jose. The man was sucking an upturned bottle, wiping his mouth with the back of his hand. "A likely pair," Samuel thought as the driver cracked his whip over the mule team and burst into a cheerful Spanish trail song.

Samuel resigned himself to wait until Susan could travel. He would have to set out on a long difficult trail unaccompanied by the train.

When Susan found that the army, the scouts and James had left the

Fort, and that Samuel was going to wait until her recovery, she brightened considerably. Though she was alone or with Jane most of each day, after supper Samuel remained with her in their room. They talked of personal things, future plans, the child they lost. At last she brought herself to ask, "Samuel, where did you bury our baby? Can I see the grave?"

He had hoped she wouldn't ask this question. Each time he entered the plaza he turned his eyes from the small insignificant mound. "When you are stronger," he said, "I'll show you."

Then he diverted her with tales about the Fort, first called Fort William after the Bent brother who had supervised most of the construction. "It opened for trade about 1833, while still incomplete. The shrewd Bent brothers applied for a government license to trade, not only with neighboring tribes like the Cheyennes and Arapahoes, but with the Snakes, Comanches, Kiowas and Sioux. This meant they would always have a dependable supply of beaver pelts and buffalo hides. Will Bent married a daughter of priest Grey Thunder, Keeper of the Arrows."

"I think I saw her in the *sala* the day we came. Isn't Bent's wife named Yellow Woman?"

"Owl Woman was his first wife. Yellow Woman became his wife when her sister died." Samuel hastily changed the subject, for he didn't want to tell Susan that Owl Woman died in childbirth.

On another night he told her a more cheerful story, one with a happy ending, a "miracle of coincidence," he called it. "The Bents had always paid ransom demanded by Indians for white captives, taken in raids on settlements and from caravans. They then in turn collected from the government when the individuals were freed. One day a wagon train pulled into the Fort with an American woman named Dale whose husband had been killed at Pawnee Fork. Her seven-year-old son Paul vanished during the fracas. Since she was closely guarded herself, she couldn't search for him. After days and weeks of terror, doubled by grief, she managed to slip out of camp and finally found a trail made by a wagon."

"Oh, the poor woman. How she must have suffered," sighed Susan.

"Well, she knew enough to keep on the trail. She knew it would lead somewhere, perhaps to a stream or spring. I'm sure she preferred death in the desert to life as a captive. After several days, more dead than alive, she was picked up by a caravan at a spot where she had collapsed. The wagonmaster revived her, made a bed of buffalo hide, gave her food and water until the trail reached Bent's Fort. William took care of her until she regained her strength. Then she was employed in the Fort kitchen."

"I know how she must have felt," said Susan. "I'm grateful Bent took us in when we needed care."

"As long as the Fort was a main stopping place for the traders, William knew that the news would spread along the routes both east and south. He assured Mrs. Dale that if the boy were still alive, word would drift back somehow. It turned out that some trappers found the child where he had hidden in the bushes and took him with them to Independence. Nobody there claimed him nor knew of any relatives. So the trappers just took him along when they made the next trip west. They hoped for word that never came."

Samuel was glad that Susan seemed absorbed in the story. "They stopped here at the Fort for provisions and, since the boy complained of hunger, a trapper called Blackfoot brought him to the kitchen for food. He asked a woman who was stirring a kettle of stew at the fireplace to feed the boy. When Mrs. Dale glanced up and saw her lost son standing before her, cries of joy filled the Fort."

"Oh, oh." Susan's eyes moistened. "You're right, it truly is a miracle. Then what happened?"

"She and the boy rode a wagon back to Missouri on the next trip."

Samuel's stories and loving attention helped Susan regain her vitality and spirits. In daily prayers she asked forgiveness for letting her love for Samuel eclipse devotion to a Higher Power. The days wore on. Jane was absent for long periods of time and Susan suspected she was spending it downstairs with the black man.

"Take me out for a little walk," she said to Samuel one night. "I need exercise."

Her request surprised him but he was pleased to see her more like herself. Delicate and pale, she was more beautiful to him than ever. She was dressed in one of her new gowns, her dark hair brushed smooth and shining as a raven's breast. The candle on their supper table softened her deep brown eyes. "We'll walk on the promenade around the parapet at the back of the fort. I want to show you a beautiful sight."

They made their way slowly. Susan paused to exclaim over the immensity of the dusty plain before them. "Each time I see the prairie from a height, I realize how much our own destiny depends upon this vast land. What a huge world it is, how little of it I have seen until now."

"Sounds like you're getting anxious to travel again." The first real smile in days lightened his eyes.

"You've been so good to me, Samuel, and I know it has been a sacrifice." Then she turned back to gaze over the land toward the wagon camp near the river. "What was it you wanted to show me?"

"Let's walk to the back of the Fort where the stock is kept during the winter in the adobe corral."

Susan wondered about his use of the word beautiful in describing anything about the mud brick Fort, the same monotonous clay color of the soil from which it was made. But she couldn't believe her eyes when she saw the tops of the wide walls blooming with thousands of crimson cactus flowers and the yellow cups of prickly pear. They made a solid ribbon of color around the corral, their spiny undergrowth guarding the wall from raiders. She gasped in delight, turning her head from side to side to take in the beauty of the waxen blossoms, now tinged rosier by the setting sun.

"The Bents thought of everything in building their Fort, didn't they?" Samuel said, delighting in her pleasure. "They made the walls unscalable with that wide bed of cactus."

With their arms entwined they lingered until the sun sank leaving an afterglow on the wide summer sky. Susan glanced up, exclaiming again with joy, "I feel as if a blue china bowl filled with fluffy pink peonies had been set over us."

Samuel looked surprised at her comparison. "I guess the clouds do look like giant flowers sometimes, but I never thought about it that way." On their return to their room, he felt his heart lift in response to her happy mood.

The next morning the tent boys, Jose, Sandoval and the Indian driver, came to her room before she had finished a late breakfast. "Mr. Samuel, he say to knock down the bed and pack up your things for you," reported Jose. "He say to stay downstairs until he brings the Dearborn around to the gate."

Though considerably surprised, Susan didn't object and soon Jane appeared to pack the basket of personal things needed during the day. Samuel came a little later to lift her into the carriage bed with Jane to ride beside her.

"All set?" he asked when she had stretched out full length with great relief. He reached into his pocket and pulled out a small pistol, watching her eyes widen in surprise and fright. "Susan, listen carefully. You know why I insisted you learn how to use a firearm when we started."

She nodded, remembering how her hand trembled on the pearl handle when they practiced shooting at a target nailed to the barn door at the farm. "You don't think I'll have to use it?" she quavered.

"In case I'm not close by, I want you to keep this gun where you can reach it. See, the safety latch is on. Don't move it around any more than you have to, but remember where you put it now." He gave her a quick kiss and jumped to the ground, hurrying off to find Captain Hall.

Susan stowed the gun in her basket at first, then decided it would be safer under her pillow. She lay back quietly, realizing as they were about to cross the Arkansas River into Mexican territory, she was

36

leaving her native land for the first time.

"Dear Lord, this is the first time, don't let it be the last. Please bring us back safely." Susan had observed enough of the Fort life to know that this year was different from all of the other years. She realized that perhaps 1846 would be remembered as a turning point of some kind and that she was a part of this history. She looked up from her pillow toward the Fort with Old Glory furling on its staff on the bell tower. Patriotism and nostalgia welled up in her eyes as the carriage rolled toward Santa Fe.

5

The monotony of the dusty plains began to break with rolling sand hills showing an endless pattern of wind ripples. But here there were no blue-green waves of grass to rise and swell, only the brittle parched leaves of an occasional bush. Susan lay comfortable and cool in the Dearborn bed where, by squinting her eyes against the glare, she viewed false ponds, mirages, in the distance.

She fished under her pillow for her well-worn copy of *Commerce of the Prairies*, but instead of the soft book binding, her fingers brushed against the pearl handle of the pistol Samuel had given her. In a quick gesture of fear, she lifted the pillow, assuring herself that the safety catch was still secure.

"What's the matter, Miss Susan? You feelin' poorly again?"

"Oh, I'm all right." She didn't want to alarm Jane and cause her to panic at the sight of the pistol near at hand. 'Just hand me the book by Mr. Gregg that is in the basket there. I want to read again what he said about mirages. I can't understand how light reflected from a prairie would cause a portion of the sky to appear below the horizon and resemble water."

"I don't understand any of that a'tall," replied Jane," but I would swear I see a blue lake not very far off. We never seem to catch up with it. Just keeps movin' ahead, real spooky like."

Susan flipped pages in the book. "Mr. Gregg says that perhaps it's gas from decaying vegetation that created the mirages. I don't know how anything could decay in this dry air – seems as if it would shrivel and blow away first." She pondered the question, wishing she knew a woman with whom she could discuss such things. If she could just receive a letter from home, she might not feel so lonesome and forgotten.

Along this dreary trail where water was always scarce, they began to drink wine with all their meals except breakfast, carefully saving the empty bottles for later trade with the Mexican villagers. Samuel was also relieved they saw no signs of danger from lurking native marauders. Susan's lethargic interest was aroused at "Hole in the Rock" where the train stopped for water. At times they traveled without stopping until nearly midnight, starting up at dawn, resting during the heat of the day. Hours of sleep and meals were erratic and hard on dispositions.

On August 12 a flaming red dawn turned into a golden morning. When Susan awoke, the first stirrings of camp caused her to sit up in bed with a sense of expectancy. She stretched her arms in an involuntary gesture toward the sun as its rays lighted up the grass, making each tuft, each seed head stand out in gilded lines. This is the day, she thought, today I will put behind me all the trouble and sorrow I've known during my illness. From now on I'll look toward Santa Fe and a better life. She turned to Jane with enthusiasm and her old bright smile warmed her face. "Hand me my new calico and help me do up my hair. I'm tired of wearing this old wrapper. Today I feel alive again!"

"Yas'm, yas'm," Jane repeated. "It's good to see you more like your old self. Mr. Samuel will be as glad as I am. He's been worried, Miss Susan, powerful worried 'bout you."

When he rode up shortly, carefully balancing tin cups and an enamel-ware pitcher filled with hot coffee, Susan greeted him with her flashing good looks. He squeezed her hand with sudden desire as he released the cup and his eyes caressed her with longing. "Oh, my Susanita, how well, how beautiful you look to me this morning!"

"I feel like myself again. Things will be better for us from now on, *mi alma*. I know everything will be all right. I'm even planning to walk about the camp a little as soon as I drink my coffee."

"Just be careful and keep Ring with you."

They were camped in pinon flats near the Purgatoire River which they had crossed without much difficulty. Susan thought it looked much like the Arkansas with banks thickly overgrown by brush and young cottonwood trees. The sight of the entrance to Raton Pass in the distance awakened a new sense of adventure. A towering rock at the very pinnacle looked to her like the rounded top of a covered wagon. She wondered about their fate among the rough stones and outcroppings strewn along the pass through the Rocky Mountains. In her imagination she peopled it with Indians and outlaws and wouldn't have been surprised to see a grizzly or a prairie wolf slipping from behind the stones. The boulders themselves were so large she wondered how wagons could possibly pass over or between. Samuel told her that the pass was named Raton for the huge pack rats that lived among the boulders.

In the next days Susan's customary walks about the camp turned into longer hikes up the mountain while they waited on inevitable wagon repairs. She examined a curiously formed pebble, black with thin stripes of white crossing its rough surface. Embedded in shallow sand she found a small shell, the empty home of a marine creature in a prehistoric sea from which the very crest of the mountain had been thrust in ages past. A bright blue feather of a Stellar jay was also tucked into her pocket collection. I must remember where I found these, she thought, and note it in my journal. She tasted the bittersweet fruit of the chokecherry, making wry faces at the astringent flavor. She bit into the soft green shells of pinon nuts, fragrant with evergreen oil.

The next day she asked Jose to saddle her horse so she could explore on her own. Ring trotted along side just out of reach of the mare's hooves. To her eyes, now accustomed to prairie distance, the height and bulk of the mountains was physically overpowering. She felt her very being shrink as she gazed at the massive strength of the rocky ledge and the vast, illimitable blue. "Oh, I will lift mup mine eyes," she quoted softly, and added a quick prayer of thanks for their continued safety.

As she turned her horse to descend, she caught a glimpse of a perfect haven, the light green fields and orchards circled by dark forms of fir and pine. Shafts of evergreen shadowed a mountain valley church. What would life be like in such a place, she wondered. Would I be happy here, living where day follows day, season after season, always the same? Would I mind being confined to one spot, ideal though it seems to me now? She had to admit that at times on the arduous journey she would have welcomed such a place of monotonous beauty, but she knew in her heart of hearts that this valley of security, like her Kentucky home, wasn't what she wanted from life. She had cast her lot with Samuel and his trail of adventure.

She pulled into the shade of a pinon pine farther down the slope to watch the tortuous descent of a wagon, wheels securely locked, teams unharnessed, that was being lowered by sweating men who pulled back against the holding ropes with all their combined strength and weight. That day the train advanced only half a mile. They camped early.

"With every smack of iron wheel-tires against those rocks I feared the wagon would break and crash down the hill," she told Samuel that night.

"Some of your fears are justified," he said grimly, "quite a few wagon tongues snapped off, a number of wheels collapsed on the rocks. We're losing time due to repair, but it can't be helped. Are you enjoying the scenery of Raton Pass? Isn't it grander than I described to you?"

"Oh, it's magnificent. I wouldn't have believed that beside these craggy heights our own green Kentucky mountains now seem dwarfed, positively small. It's overpowering. Yet there's always another crag that looms higher and higher."

The moon, hidden by clouds, suddenly cast a luminous glow upon the tent, the sleeping oxen and their masters. From a campfire not too distant they heard the soft chords of Comapu's battered guitar. His boyish voice lifted in tribute to the beauty of the night.

La Noche esta serena,   *the night is serene,*
Todo en silencio esta   *all is in silence.*

"I wish," mused Samuel, "that he had always confined his singing to the campfire. Oh my dearest, if only I could have stopped those runaway mules. If only I could have spared you."

"Let's not dwell on it any longer. It's over and past; as much as I grieve, too, I want to think only of our future from now on."

Samuel reached over to gather her tenderly in his arms, "My darling, don't you know what you mean to me?" His lips sought hers. With an eagerness that sent his heart pounding, she responded to his kisses and caresses.

On the 18th of August, the Magoffin wagons, being newly repaired, were ready to resume their journey to Santa Fe. A cold rain with the foretaste of autumn made the already dangerous road completely impassable. Before noon another company of soldiers arrived at the camp to fortify their safe advance into the ancient city. But instead of being assured by their presence, the company of traders became more apprehensive and uncertain. They had heard rumors of grass being burned by the Mexican ranchers fleeing before the advancing army. If this were true, there would be no forage for teams during the remainder of their journey. Exaggerated tales of armed resistance along the route created fear for both their lives and their goods.

The Magoffins were enjoying a quiet meal under their tent when a courier in blue uniform of the Army of the West rode up and dismounted in deep mud. "Magoffin," he called. "Lt. Warner reporting with a message from Brigadier-General Kearny, sir."

Samuel started up hurriedly, nearly upsetting their bowls of meat stew on the folding table. "Brigadier-General Kearny? Did you hear that Susan? The Colonel has been promoted!" He dabbed at his mouth with a large napkin and looked expectantly at the handsome officer standing at attention. Susan waited discreetly inside the tent door until the message was delivered. She watched her husband's face, knowing that his expression would reveal the meaning, even if she couldn't hear the low-toned conversation.

"I bring greetings from General Kearny to both you and Mrs. Magoffin. He hopes that her health is improving."

Samuel read the message quickly and the tension in his face relaxed a little as he stuffed the paper in his pocket. "Come in, share our meal, Lieutenant. Susan will be happy to visit with you." He pulled back the tent flap in a gesture of hospitality.

Warner, just a few years older than Susan, admired her with the frank enthusiasm of a bachelor soldier a long way from home. He stepped inside, bowed low over her extended hand, then let his keen eyes quickly take in the comfort of their little prairie house. "I wouldn't have believed it, sir, unless I had seen this for myself. But of course for a lady like your beautiful wife –" He paused to watch Susan's cheeks redden.

"Won't you share our meal?" she asked.

"There's nothing I'd rather do, but I must attend to the repair of the road this afternoon or else none of the wagons will make it to Santa Fe. The rains have made a bad road worse. Will you be sending a return message, sir?"

"No, just inform the General that we'll be ready to move, either way, upon further word from him. And tell my brother if you see him that all is well with the wagon train. Also tell him," Samuel paused to choose words that James only would understand, "that we toast his success."

With a salute to Samuel, a bow to Susan, Lt. Warner stepped outside the warm tent into a slow drizzle of cold rain. "Tell me, tell me, what did the General say in his letter? Did he mention James? What did you mean by saying that we would move, *either way?*"

"Susanita, don't be so excited. The General merely stated that negotiations between James and Governor Armijo were proceeding. He said that he had entered Las Vegas on the 15th, over three days ago. He has taken possession of all New Mexico territory as a friend and protector against Texas claims, not as a conqueror. In addition Mexican forces were said to be assembling at Apache Canyon."

"Was that *all* he wrote?" Susan said.

"He mentioned that if the army advance was stopped at the canyon, he would send word for the wagon trains to retreat to safety within U.S. borders under military escort."

"You mean we would have to go back? This close to Santa Fe? Back over that dreadful Raton Pass?"

41

"You ask too many questions at once, Pet." He added, "If Kearny's forces were held up, perhaps suffering military losses, we're lucky we're still this close to the U.S. border. Climbing the pass isn't quite as difficult as descending, but both are hard enough, I admit."

"Well, at least we're the last in line now, due to our late start from the Fort. That means we'd be the first to leave, if that's any comfort."

Then Samuel took the General's letter, twisted the paper and thrust it into the flame of the table lamp. When it caught, he carried it to the open door and crushed it in the mud under his heel. "From now on, be careful what you write in your journal, Pet. It would be a disaster if it fell into Mexican hands just before James had concluded his mission."

Sudden alarm clouded Susan's dark eyes, but her husband patted her cheek with a reassuring gesture. "Don't worry, I'm counting on Jim to convince Governor Armijo that to put up resistance against the U.S. forces would be disastrous and foolish. He'll have to use all his powers of persuasion, but he has plenty of blarney when he needs it."

Adhering to Samuel's warning, Susan restricted the entries in her journal to descriptions of the scenery and the usual difficulties of travel.

Wednesday, 18th of August

Out of the Raton at last! We have been in it five days and it seem-ed that we were never to leave it. This morning the pulling has been worse than ever; some very steep, long, rocky hills, but we passed them without an accident save the breaking of two or three wagon bows — this cannot be considered an accident any more --

Susan also noted that the crisp nights of late August in high altitude were like true autumn "back home." The tent was chilly, even with double blankets and a heavy quilt. She was well again; filled with an-ticipation of Santa Fe; she was happy to have Samuel, solicitous and lov-ing, always at her side.

Next morning the train approached the steep, slick banks of Poni Creek which had been made worse by steady rain through the night. Samuel, with Captain Hall's help, selected a place farther down where a bend in the creek provided a shallow ford. A dry, rocky area lay between it and the second loop of the horseshoe bend which also had level banks. The entire group of wagons could be easily sent over this safer, though double, crossing.

The Magoffins rode in the lead on horseback and were met on the far side by Lt. Warner, who was still superintending road repair for the advancing army and traders. "May I wish you a good morning?" he said with an appreciative smile in Susan's direction as he doffed his military cap with a wider sweep than was customary.

"Top o' the morning to you too, Lieutenant," replied Samuel lapsing into Irish brogue. "How's the road farther on? Is it as muddy as this?"

"We're doing our best, sir. Rayado Creek is flowing bank full at present, too full to ford."

"It'll be noon tomorrow before we have to cross at that place. Just now I need to go back to guide the wagons over. Will you help Susan select a proper camp site for tonight? I'll send the tent boys and baggage wagon over as soon as I can."

"Yes, sir, my pleasure, sir." The Lieutenant replied with such obvious enthusiasm that Susan cast a questioning glance in his direction.

What is Samuel thinking of, sending that flirty officer to help me? I'm capable of choosing a proper place. Susan fumed inwardly at the situation which would place Warner so uncomfortably close to her. She hoped Jose and Sandoval would be quick crossing over, for she didn't want to sit on horseback and engage in idle chatter that might lead to an embarrassing situation. How different I feel now that I am married, she confessed to herself. Or do I want to be tempted by flattering masculine attention as I once did? Am I afraid of my own feminine response?

She spoke more crisply to Warner than before: "Lieutenant, I'll have no trouble selecting a place. See, there's level ground large enough for our four wagons and carriage just down the creek. Do not let me detain you, sir. I'm capable myself."

Lt. Warner was taken back at her coolness. He hadn't expected her to be so independent. "But Mrs. Magoffin, your husband --"

"Never mind, I prefer to do this myself," she said shortly, feeling a hot flush creep over her cheeks as he continued to stare at her. She knew she was being rude, but he made her uncomfortable. His flirtatious glances had awakened her 19-year-old heart. At home she might have engaged in a light flirtation for the challenge of it, but here on the trail, with an army man, never. She couldn't bring herself even to smile back. She wondered if she could really trust her emotions if he pressed his attentions another time.

Warner doffed his cap, and Susan noticed a hurt, puzzled expression in his blue eyes as he turned away. "As you wish, Madam," he said in a low tone and cut his horse quickly with his whip.

As soon as he had ridden away, she found a suitable place, dismounted and walked around to find the least muddy location for the tent. Jose and Sandoval came up shortly and she directed them, half in English, half in Spanish, sharing their smiles at her awkwardness with their musical language. She managed to indicate the location by repeating several times, "*Tienda aqui*, tent here, *tienda aqui.*"

When she had time to look around, she discovered what she thought was snow on the highest peak. Snow in August, she wondered in surprise. Back home they're sweltering in dreadful humidity. Oh, this country is different from any place I've ever been before. She got out the map to find that they must cross three more creeks, Rayado, Ocate and Mora, before they came to the first Mexican settlement. Until there was further word from General Kearny, the train would proceed south as planned.

Her next diary entry on August 25th described the small village of Mora as being mud hovels, each surrounded by a fence of tall irregular sticks, an *estaca* which no predator, animal or human could climb. The *rancheros* made their living by raising cattle, beans, chili and squash – *vacas, frijoles, chili* and *calabazas*, she added to practice writing in Spanish. In her opinion, living in such a manner was probably a miserable existence, but the people looked content, smiling and laughing.

The next day they made camp at the *vegas* or meadows, a high rolling grassland of incomparable beauty. Instead of Susan enjoying the unusual sights of the settlement, she herself proved to be the greatest attraction. As she waited alone in the carriage with a sheer veil over her face, she soon realized that the simple folk gathered curiously around her had never before seen a Rockaway carriage or a well-dressed American lady of white complexion. "Stop laughing," she whispered in a low tone to Samuel "Stop encouraging them. If you were a good business man you could charge them a *peso* to look at me." She had to smile back in spite of herself at the naive amazement of the village children who stared at her and cried loudly, "*gringa, gringa!*"

Most of the younger children were completely naked while the larger ones both boys and girls, wore only a short, dirty shirt. They chattered in such rapid Spanish that Susan couldn't understand what they were saying but knew it was about her. "Speak to them, Susan. They're just curious, like any other children. They mean no harm by staring."

"*Buenos dias, como estan!* Good day, how are you?" Her reply to her husband's suggestion brought shrieks of delight from the children. "*Gringa, gringa, hable espanol!* American woman speaks Spanish!" they shouted. A few boys, made bold by her pleasant manner, tried to climb the high step of her carriage. Adults too crowded nearer, eyeing Susan and gesturing. Even the numerous village dogs added to the general excitement with staccato barking that rose above the din of voices.

In a moment Jose returned and directed them into the front room in a tiny adobe house whose owner was accustomed to providing food for the traders in exchange for small household items from their wagon supplies. As many of the curious crowd as could squeezed into the room and stood about the walls, watching the table where the Americans were seated. Susan looked them over too, but tried not to stare as directly as they did.

Hombres in loose cotton trousers pushed back their woven straw hats as they stood, quietly shifting their weight on bare brown feet that showed mud stains from the fields. *Mujeres* wearing blue cotton *camisas* and full *faldas*, some with noisily nursing babies under their *rebozas*, followed Susan's every movement with inquisitive dark eyes. Satisfied that the white strangers would not vanish, both men and women brought out tobacco pouches, rolled and lighted small *cigarritos*. Soon the air was murky with acrid smoke that hovered thickly over the room. The windows were too small and too closed up with humanity for much ventilation. Susan's eyes smarted from the fumes and she coughed but, noting a warning look from her husband, she stopped. Very patiently they waited until at last an old man shuffled from the kitchen with a folded blanket and a less than white tablecloth which he carefully smoothed upon the table. Then to protect the dingy cover, he placed a dirty top cloth over it. He did not supply knives, forks or spoons, much less napkins or glasses of water. Although Susan's nose tilted a little in disdain, she made no audible comments. At intervals her husband and the trader friend who had joined them spoke half in Spanish and half in English so that their curious audience couldn't follow their line of thought. To them the conversation sounded very friendly.

Soon the old man returned with a plate of flat *tortillas* made from blue Indian corn meal, a hunk of smelly, mold-speckled cheese and an earthen pot of meat stew. "How are we going to eat this?" Susan whispered.

"Just watch and do as I do," Samuel answered, reaching for a *tortilla* that he folded over twice so that the edges formed a shallow scoop. This he dipped into the common pot, fishing up chunks of meat, green chili and onions. But he wasn't quite quick enough. Liquid dripped through his fingers onto the grimy top layer of the table covers.

Susan watched, then clumsily folded a *tortilla* likewise, dipped in and managed to get some stew balanced on the edge. As soon as she placed it in her mouth, however, her eyes fairly bulged from the unexpected fiery taste. Quick tears rimmed her lids, the strong odor ticked her nose. She sneezed loudly. Her mouth burned as if consumed by fire. "*Agua, por favor,*" she managed to gasp, "*agua,* water please."

Again Samuel shook his head at her, and she gamely tried another bite or two, realizing that now every eye in the room was watching. He, in particular, seemed amused, and she was furious, burning as much from personal indignation as from the hot chili. Finally, taking pity on her plight, he spoke to the cook, "*Huevos por la senora.*"

Susan knew that he had ordered eggs and determined she would eat them in whatever form they were served. Hard fried eggs were not an especial delicacy, but she had no choice. When at last Samuel began digging into his pocket for pesos, she rose from the table with a very audible sigh and headed toward the door. The silent crowd parted to let the Americans pass. They seemed fascinated by Susan's fancy bonnet and veil and the black shawl with silken fringe that swayed as she walked. One tiny girl reached out to grasp her full skirt as she swung by. *"Bonita, bonita,* pretty, pretty." Susan couldn't resist the brown-eyed child and patted her head, not knowing whether the compliment was given for her dress or herself. For her husband's sake she managed to keep a stiff smile on her face, even though she was shaken by the experience and still very hungry.

When they were seated in the carriage, Samuel turned to her and spoke sternly. "Susan, don't you realize that you are a foreigner to those people? You're in *their* homeland, not back in the states, and the two countries are at *war.* Please be careful not to offend by word or manner."

Susan interrupted him with an impatient gesture. "Couldn't you see that I was miserable trying to swallow that hot stuff? I don't care who was looking, it was terrible."

"Well, you'll have to learn to eat it because chili is always served in Mexican homes. Remember, *hase lo que veres* -- do as they do. In Santa Fe the service won't be so crude, but the food will be just as hot."

Susan flushed at this rebuke from the usually patient and loving Samuel. She recalled conversations between her mother and her older sister Anna who had also married a Magoffin. Now she understood what her mother meant by saying that "no woman holds all of any man."

The trader Soloman Houck had said nothing during the interchange between husband and wife, but he probably would have agreed with Samuel if asked. Only last night he had heard Captain Hall questioning a Mexican spy who had been found hiding in the brush near the camp. It was discovered from his confused answers that the native *rancheros* were just as afraid of the American army as the traders were apprehensive of the Mexicans. "Americanos keel, take *mujeres, muchachos,"* he had muttered. "Padre say soldiers take slaves, drive off *vacas,* burn *campos* and *adobes."* He gestured wildly about with outspread arms toward the landscape. When asked about the soldiers, the frightened spy lifted his shoulders in a Spanish shrug and again waved toward the hills. "Most *hombres* go back to *casas,* some stay with General Armijo."

Leaving Las Vegas, Samuel and Susan rode in silence through the dusty heat of the afternoon, each busy with thoughts over the coming events as they approached Santa Fe. Houck again rode up to report that the Pueblo Indians were not joining forces with the Mexican government as the traders had feared. "We have just learned from an outrider that the northern tribes feel the coming of the pale skins is a fulfillment of an ancient prophesy," he cried with satisfaction.

"Thank God for that," exclaimed Samuel with obvious relief as he reached over to pat Susan's hand. "He means that the Pueblos expect the Americans to deliver them from years of Spanish oppression and restore the ancient kingdom of Montezuma."

Susan managed to smile at his gesture of reconciliation. "Who was Montezuma?" she asked politely.

"A pueblo chieftain who built a temple about 300 years ago. Legend says that when the pueblo became overcrowded, Montezuma moved southward, establishing other villages for his people as he went. Eventually he is said to have founded what is now Mexico City."

"James told me about a sacred fire. Was it at this pueblo?" she asked.

"That's the story. Montezuma is supposed to have lighted it in the underground *estufa* and decreed that twelve virgins should be selected to gather wood and tend the flame until his return. They felt honored to be chosen for this holy task. As the years passed, others took their places. The story goes that evil spirits descended upon the group who guarded the altar flame and caused them to sink into such a deep slumber that the fire went out. After that the people were frightened and abandoned the pueblo. Montezuma never returned to lead his people against the hated Spanish, but the legend is that they would be delivered at the hands of a pale face people from the East. We'll pass by the ruined city and stop long enough for you to see it. Some years ago on a trading trip I spent the night in a partially ruined casa. One of the Indians living there allowed me to stay during a heavy storm."

"You never told me that before!" Samuel's story seemed to rekindle Susan's sense of adventure, her eyes shone in anticipation. "This trip, ever since Bent's Fort, has been a trip through history for me."

He looked at her intently at the mention of the Fort, but if she still had pangs of remorse, her expression didn't reveal them. Perhaps, he mused, she really meant what she said about putting the sad events of the past behind her.

Since they were now approaching a stand of tall pines and pinon shrubs, he gave orders to halt their carriage and baggage wagons for the night. He began to hope that their entry into Santa Fe would be peaceful after all. That is, if the spy's story about the Mexican forces deserting Armijo could be believed.

Samuel moved about the camp, breathing air scented with the fragrance of pinon. Small branches and logs were smouldering into coals for cooking the evening meal. Ring and Jane had followed Susan on one of her exploring trips and the tent hands sang at their work.

Familiar words of "Juanita," a favorite Spanish song, echoed clearly over the ripple of a mountain stream. This night Samuel was filled with content and a growing sense of security. His heart lightened at the thought of easy entry into Santa Fe under the American flag.

Next morning Susan sensed the change in his mood and chattered with enthusiasm about the scenery and Mexican settlements they were passing through. As they approached the creek near San Miguel, she suddenly gasped and began to rummage in the basket.

"What's the matter, need something?" asked Samuel, startled at her haste.

"My veil, my veil," she answered. "Just look at that crowd of naked children splashing in the water. Boys and girls—have they no modesty?"

Samuel guffawed at her blushes and the deft movements of her hands in tying a double thickness of veil over her eyes. "If those naked children disturb you, take a look at the mothers."

The women who were engaged in washing themselves and their *muchachos* in the shallow water splashed boisterously about, their full skirts pulled way above their knees, their blouses lowered off their brown shoulders gleaming wetly in the sun.

Susan turned her head ever so slightly so that any man in the wagon train following them would not think she was staring. "Oh, they're not wearing underclothes at all. You can even see their *bare bosoms* when they lean over."

"Quite a sight, isn't it?" Samuel grinned. "Why take a bath with all their clothes on? Beside, I doubt if they own any underwear."

"I still think it's shocking to look at such sights in the presence of the men. My mother would die of shame if she were here!"

"This isn't Kentucky, Susan," Samuel chuckled.

Later that day she forgot all about her embarrassment when a messenger arrived with the electrifying news that Governor Armijo had actually fled Santa Fe; that General Kearny had taken possession of the Governor's Palace and of the city itself; that all the lands held by Mexico clear to the *west coast* were now claimed by the U.S. Army.

As the news spread, pandemonium broke out in the camp. Wagoners and teamsters, drivers and wranglers raced crazily about, whooping and cheering. "Hooray for the army! Hooray for General Kearny! Hooray for the red, white and blue!" Samuel watched as bottles of whiskey were passed around but he moved to stand by his own wagons of expensive liquors lest the men get too boisterous in their celebration. "Well, James apparently succeeded in persuading Governor Armijo not to fight, but I'd sure like to know how he did it, I really would."

"Do you suppose he'll tell us when we get to Santa Fe?" she asked, joy and relief showing in her face.

"I'll certainly give him ample opportunity to explain. However I doubt if the details will ever be known, certainly not printed in future history books."

After breaking camp at San Miguel where they had been welcomed with gifts of food and a skin of goat's milk, they traveled at a brisk pace. The grandeur of the mountain peaks matched their morning mood of exhiliration.

True to his promise, Samuel halted his carriage long enough to ride horseback with Susan up to the ruined village of Pecos. "This used to be one of the largest of the pueblos," he told her, "but death from disease and raiding Comanches dwindled the population. I've heard only 17 souls remained in 1838 when they finally decided to join the tribe in the Jemez Mountains."

He led her over the fallen stones and desolate adobe foundations where families had lived and worked. "Just think," she mused aloud, "my horse is standing in the middle of someone's home. What a pity these proud people had to abandon it to the elements."

Soon they dismounted near the church built to Catholic specifications by the Spanish padres who came after Coronado. Another set of ruins of early Aztec origin lay close by. "It was in this *estufa*," Samuel pointed to an excavation nearly 40 feet wide, "that the sacred fire was lighted by Montezuma and kept burning for generations."

Susan stooped to pick up a shard of decorated pottery. "I'll add this to my collection," she said, turning the sun-warmed fragment in her hand. "I wish I knew who made this – maybe she was a young woman like me, maybe this was a pot to hold the cornmeal she ground. You know, *mi alma*, just standing here where others lived so long ago makes me feel kin to all people, makes me realize that we were created by One Great Father, red people, white people as well as brown and black. Their God is our God."

"You're right, my dear, we are only two small pieces in His great plan and we must try to fulfill our destinies as best we can while we remain in this world." She wasn't used to such a profound statement from her practical trader husband, but she realized that years of travel over this area must have created in him a sense of history and appreciation of the earth and its peoples.

They wandered about the church; the adobe walls were still partly intact. Susan surveyed the great dimension of the ruins and the intricate pattern in which the bricks were laid. Large pine vigas were carved in Aztec figures as were the massive door and altar. "How did they learn to do these things?" she asked in wonderment. "I thought that the early people were ignorant."

"That's a common misconception in the States. These Indians were uneducated by white man's standards, but they were ingenious people. They had the same innate ability to get along that we do. Considering they had only tools of their own making, the pueblo people were outstanding artisans and craftsmen."

She gazed at the ruins of many small adobe huts clustered at various distances around the old mission church. "Show me the place where you slept out the storm."

He stepped over fallen rubble to indicate a wall with a high window opening and a partial door framework. "See where the door was hung on that rotting timber? It was the entry to a second story room which I reached by climbing an outside ladder."

Susan loked at the tumbled adobe bricks and marveled at the coincidence that had brought her to this primitive place. "Were the people really friendly to the white man then?"

"Yes, traders and their wagons were gradually welcomed in the peaceful pueblos like Pecos. But remember, that wasn't too long ago, and there was no war then like the troubled times we're living in now."

As they rode back to camp Susan saw for the first time a number of *senoritas*, their faces covered with a thick white flour paste which gave them a most startling appearance. "Look, why do those young girls have their faces smeared? They look like ghosts."

He chuckled as he answered. "Oh, women will do anything to make themselves beautiful. Vanity was planted in the breast of Eve and females have been searching for beauty ever since."

"So they call smeared faces attractive?" She watched the girls swinging arm and arm toward the village, their full skirts moving in graceful ripples as they walked.

"See, they're dressed in their best and are probably going to a fandango tonight. The flour paste bleaches their dark skins, and they think they'll be more attractive to dance partners if they look a little different from usual. They'll wash it off before the music starts. Sometimes they smear red paste over their cheeks and this stays on until it wears off."

"Well, I'm glad I don't have to whiten my face that way. It probably needs bleaching after so many weeks in the open sunshine," she replied. "I'll be glad when we can stay long enough in Santa Fe for me to care for my skin and hair," She touched her cheeks lightly and frowned. "My face feels so dry and rough – I'm afraid this climate has given me crow's feet and wrinkles."

Her husband laughed again. "You women are all alike, regardless of the color of your skins. Captain Hall told me this morning that this would be our last day out, so tomorrow we'll see Santa Fe. Then you'll have time to repair the trail damage.''

6

Susan turned restlessly in her sleep that night, finally waking Samuel who mumbled, ''What's the matter, are you ill?''

''No, too excited to sleep,'' she whispered, ''excited to see for myself all the sights, the sounds, even the smells of Santa Fe.''

''There'll be plenty of time for you to see it all, go to sleep now.'' He pulled their covers a little higher against the chilly mountain air that seeped into the tent.

''Don't you realize that I'll really be the first American woman to journey this far by wagon train? Of course there were hardships, but I've made it –'' She paused, then whispered again, ''we've made it together, dearest, just as we planned. That's what's important to me.''

''I feel thankful, too, every time I reach Santa Fe. This time especially, since you're along,'' he answered. He put an arm around her shoulder. ''Sleep now, please dear, tomorrow is almost here.''

At first flush of dawn the camp began to stir as if some of Susan's own excitement had been transferred to each dog, each mule and each teamster. Tantalizing whiffs of pinon smoke, coffee and bacon made Susan jump from bed, calling eagerly to Jane for help in dressing.

''Yas'm, Miss Susan, you want to primp already yet?''

''I want my second best black dress, Jane, my best bonnet and veil. I want to look like a proper American lady when I come in sight of Old Glory. Samuel says he wants us to salute the flag General Kearny hoisted over the Governor's Palace. And get me a fresh handkerchief to wave!''

Jane grinned at her mistress' youthful enthusiasm. ''I'm gettin' mighty anxious myself, Miss Susan. It's been a heap long time since we started from home.''

After breakfast the whole camp engaged in preparation for the grand

51

entry of *la caravana*. The stock was brushed of mud and bits of weeds. Teamsters fixed their leather "crackers" to the ends of their whips so that the sharp popping sounds would bring curious villagers running from their adobe huts: *"Los Americanos aqui; los Americanos!"*

Bright goods such as flashy tin ware, calico and looking glasses were repacked at the back of several wagons for the quick attraction of eager customers. Clouds of trail dust were shaken from wrinkled trousers; leather and corduroy jackets brushed; woven ties, scarcely worn since last June, were knotted by hurrying fingers. Great blobs of shaving lather covered grizzled faces while joking wagoners took turns trimming each other's shaggy, unkempt hair and beards. "It's always best to spruce up a bit," cautioned Captain Hall. "It encourages business, especially with the ladies of the *gente fina.*"

There was never a brighter morning than August 30, 1846 when all was in readiness and the troops, the wagons and straggling livestock herds started on the last lap of the long dusty trail toward the City of Holy Faith. Sun-etched clumps of pinons stood out in sharp relief against the eye-blinding, rocky slopes of the foothills. Rabbit-brush chamisa clustered in the dry arroyos sent up pungent, bitter fragrance when heavy wheels powdered its stalks in crossing. The circling rims of the Sangre de Cristo range seemed to beckon the hastening wagons toward their evening's destination.

All day the train plodded along after the troops and it was twilight when the Magoffins' carriage reached the still-crowded plaza. Above the shouts of teamsters and the bugle commands to soldiers, the mellow tones of church bells summoned the faithful to mass. A few devout souls turned reluctantly away from the traders' wares, but most of the crowd remained to watch and buy.

For over 200 years, this same dusty plaza had been the center of life, military and civilian. Government news from Mexico City was proclaimed in front of a humble adobe structure called the Governor's Palace. From its flat roof and parapet, the Pueblo Indians, in their revolt against Spanish rule in 1680, had hurled stones and arrows at their attackers. Here the processions of the faithful marched during fiestas with lighted pine-knot torches. Sometimes the Governor's carriage and team waited in front of the Palace for his hour of afternoon driving.

The other three sides of the plaza were lined with shops and small houses. Nearby, ridged-bark cottonwood trees provided summer shade for the tethered mounts of newly-arrived soldiers. Pack burros and village wood gatherers lounged around waiting for tardy customers.

Susan noticed the fires of low-stacked logs called *luminarias*, lighting the dark, winding streets. The flames brightened the dull adobe walls. She gazed about in astonishment. "This is Santa Fe? This tiny village is hardly larger than Las Vegas. Is it really a capitol city?"

"Oh, there's more. It's too dark to see the huts down by the river as well as larger homes of the *ricos* built up the hill. The Guadalupe Church is a little distance to the west, and the paroquia at the end of San Francisco street. Of course there are no public school buildings. Dona Tules' monte parlor is just down the street from the Palace."

Samuel pointed to another cluster of adobe buildings, scarcely visible in the evening light. "Merchants sell from their wagons here or in rented stalls. Some of the Indians bargain in the streets but mostly spread out their wares on the ground beside the Palace. Large sums of money change hands here during the summer trading season."

In the gathering dusk she noticed the U.S. flag flying high over the Palace and pulled at her husband's sleeve. "Our salute, did you forget?" Solemnly they raised their hands together. In her mind she saw the flag over the old courthouse in Danville, Kentucky. How far from home is the flag of our country, she thought.

"Jim ought to turn up soon," Samuel said. "He promised before he left Bent's Fort that he would engage a house for us near the plaza."

Susan was suddenly very weary. "I hope he comes. I feel as limp as Jane's dish rag."

Like a leprechaun, Irish Jim appeared from nowhere, making his way through the crowd in the same jaunty manner he had left the Fort. "Don Santiago, Don Santiago!" cried some men to their trader friend as they pushed toward him. They knew that he usually had a bottle of wine for the man who brought the most customers to the Magoffin wagons.

"*Como esta*, Romero? *Como*, Arturo?" He informally laid an arm over their shoulders. "Come with me. I want to introduce you to someone," James advanced through the crush of wagons, people and animals. He mischievously wanted to watch his friends' reactions when they first glimpsed a white woman, a *gringa Americana*, and he also wanted to see how Susan would respond to them.

Taking Samuel by complete surprise, Jim stepped on the carriage wheel, leaned over and clapped his brother on the back. Then he swept off his Mexican hat to Susan. "Welcome to Santa Fe, you two. Mr. and Mrs. Samuel Magoffin, meet my friends Romero and Arturo. They're going to help me get you settled in the casa I've rented." He spoke as casually as if he had seen them only yesterday.

Samuel reached down to shake hands with the men while Susan nodded politely, remembering her husband's admonition in Las Vegas. She felt the men staring and knew her cheeks were as red as the fires that flickered over the scene.

James took hold of the bridle of the lead mule. "I'll guide you over. Your place is just across the alameda toward the church."

Susan was grateful to know that they would be spending the night within secure adobe walls instead of in the tent. Her woman's heart lifted at the news of a casa all her own – her very first real home with the man she loved.

With characteristic generosity James had planned a celebration supper, offering them champagne, canned oysters and crackers. After two glasses of the wine, Susan grew drowsy and excused herself. The Magoffin brothers, however, sat up late, discussing the developments of Jim's secret meeting with Governor Armijo.

"I need to know what took place," Samuel said. "I could scarcely believe the news that Kearny had entered Santa Fe without bloodshed. I knew then it must be due to some of your Irish shenanigans."

"Matter of fact, I really didn't have to pull off anything. I thought it proper to let Captain Cooke, being a representative of the U.S. Army make the first move. Even though he was well received when we met in Las Vegas on August 9 with the Alcalde, we learned upon our arrival here on the 12th that both citizens and soldiers had been alerted by the Alcalde's letter to Governor Armijo. A fairly large crowd gathered to organize a force to resist our advance –"

"We heard the same thing by courier," said Samuel.

"We proceeded with caution to the Palace under a white flag. Since our escort of only 12 men seemed too insignificant for serious conquest, we weren't molested when we asked Captain Ortiz, the Mayor, to request an audience with the Governor."

"How did Armijo receive the husband of his departed cousin, Maria Gertrudes?"

"Oh, he recognized me, lifted his eyebrows, but didn't speak personally. I took no part in the first conversation as I thought it best for an impartial interpreter to introduce Captain Cooke when he presented our credentials. Armijo shifted his eyes in my direction once or twice, especially when Cooke asked for a later meeting when the Governor's pressing business had been concluded. He seemed to question my presence there."

"I bet he was wondering what the hell you were there for."

"We came back at 10 o'clock that same night. Armijo, handsome cuss that he is, tried to impress us with all the splendor of his full dress uniform, fancy gold lace and red sash. I'd swear that his chest was lined with every medal he owned. He wore his sword in an ornamental scabbard, and his plumed helmet was on a desk nearby. All the candles were lighted, his silver and crystal decanters and goblets freshly polished and all the mirrors in the room reflected their brilliance. Cooke and I had shaved and washed off the worst of the trail dust, but we felt shabby beside this splendid Governor."

Samuel managed a wry smile at Jim's description.

"When Cooke showed them Kearny's letter and proclamation, we watched the Governor's face as he listened to its reading. He seemed taken aback by the United States' claim of *all Mexican territory* east of the Rio Grande. But I think he was bluffing. He's bound to have known about Kearny's previous proclamation at Bent's Fort which was sent to Taos. He surely realized that this claim would cut his province in two. His fingers kept drumming the table impatiently, but Archuleta seemed more incensed over the proposition than Armijo. I remember that he asked about the number of men under Kearny's command. After a while the Governor stated that he would send a commissioner back with Cooke at dawn and that he himself would lead a force of 6,000 men to negotiate with the approaching Army of the West."

"Six thousand?" queried Samuel. "Did you believe that?"

"Not quite. I knew he was given to exaggeration. He probably might have mustered 600, if the truth be known. This was a fairly tense moment, and I didn't want the old boy to get his fighting britches on before I'd had my say. I broke the tension by making a gesture toward his decanter and we all filled up. Now the time had come for me to persuade him. I appealed to his vanity, and that's considerable, by saying that he would be forced into a hopeless contest with the powerful U.S. army, a contest he couldn't win, but that if he relinquished all claim to the disputed land, he could at least retain self-respect by remaining an undefeated General. He knew that I knew the confused state of revolution with which the Mexico City government was plagued. He guessed correctly that what inadequate support he might have would be too slow in coming to his defense. He was faced with the immediate invasion by American forces already on the march toward Santa Fe."

"Yes, yes, I know all that as well as you do. What I'm curious about is the *clincher*. What did you really offer him?"

"Well, most of that has to remain a military secret," said Jim with a smile and a shrug as he drained the last drop of champagne from his glass. "But you understand that my broad hints about arranging for him to collect tariffs on all the caravans following the army might have impressed him as being a wiser course of action than armed resistance. Sometimes self-preservation is stronger than patriotism. At any rate, Armijo seemed worried. He made out his will the very next day, August 14, the day *before* Kearny read his proclamation in Las Vegas and four days before the army actually entered Santa Fe. Armijo was preparing himself for the worst. Archuleta wanted to fight and had already raised troops, but Armijo made the final decision not to resist the army."

Samuel looked at his brother with unembarrassed admiration, "Jim, you kissed the blarney stone on that one. For my sake and Susan's I'm relieved it turned out well. May the luck of the Irish continue to follow you."

"And how is the bride of the Santa Fe trail faring – after Bent's Fort, I mean."

"Remarkably well, I'd say, She's a plucky one, that Susan – loyal as they come too."

"I'd like to know her better," James said, "but I leave tomorrow night for the settlements of the *Rio Abajo* down river to pave the way for Kearny's advance into Chihuahua. You know about that don't you?"

"Enough to know that you might lose your head if it doesn't work. Before I turn in, tell me about Kearny's entrance. All we heard was that he had taken the city. How did he do it?"

"Well, the commissioner that Governor Armijo sent back with Captain Cooke the next morning to deal with the General was no other than our trader friend, Henry Connelly. He told me how the little short general mounted the roof of a house on the plaza to read his proclamation of occupation. He declared the people had become citizens of the United States and that *he* was their Governor, not Armijo. You should have heard how Connelly described the scene. It's hard to believe that the change over took place in such a short time – while the troops were watering their horses, he said. Those Mexicans had very little idea of what Kearny meant, even though his remarks were interpreted. The *Alcalde* was urged, very strongly, to swear allegiance, and when he hung his head in order not to look at Kearny – so great was his shame and confusion – he was sternly told to stand up at attention. Kearny then proclaimed him their leader and all the other citizens of the U.S government which would protect them from their enemies, provide justice for all and uphold their religion and customs."

"Go on," urged Samuel, "was Kearny acting on specific instructions from the President?"

"Only on the general understanding that if the take-over had been bloodless, he was to establish a temporary civil government and retain all exisiting officers, for instance, the Alcalde, who remained friendly.

"The same official ceremony was repeated at the villages of Tecolote and San Miguel before the army advanced to meet the expected Mexican forces at Apache Pass. But not a soldier nor rifle could be seen. Not a one, not a damn one! Fifteen miles from Santa Fe Kearny came upon the narrow pass deserted by Armijo's soldiers where only felled pine trees blocked the way. That pass could have been defended indefinitely and the army might have met a second Thermopylae if Armijo had stayed to fight. But he didn't, he fled, he vanished into nowhere."

Samuel shook his head in disbelief. "I couldn't accept this account as true from any one but you."

"Well, the General's final entry into Santa Fe plaza was almost an anti-climax, since it was a repetition of reading the proclamation and the swearing of allegiance, a procedure which very few could understand anyway. People didn't grasp the significance. Lt. Governor Vigil received General Kearny because Armijo was well on his way south with a hundred loyal dragoons. The booming cannon salute and raising the U.S. flag over the Palace at sundown on the 18th provided the biggest show in the whole ceremony, unless it was the gleam of upraised sabers."

"None of this could have taken place if the people hadn't been unhappy and oppressed by Mexican extortion and corruption anyway," commented Samuel. "They're fatalistic about misfortune. Armijo probably couldn't have counted on their undivided loyalty because the lower classes instinctively resent anyone in authority."

James again took up his story. "Kearny later claimed all the Mexican territory, millions of acres, north to the Arkansas River as well as west clear to California. I guess he reasoned that since he held the Mexican capital city he had a fair claim to the total lands under its government. You might say that the majority of citizens didn't object. It really didn't matter to them how much unoccupied land was claimed. The ruling class, however, understood it was slightly illegal and became quite unhappy with the idea. I pray that the army advance into Chihuahua will go as well. It will complete the U.S. take-over."

"In that prayer, I join you," answered Samuel, "but now I think I'd better join my wife. We're both glad to be with you, Jim, even for so short a time."

"I think I'll just bunk here on the floor," said the older brother. He pulled a wool stuffed cushion from the banco and covered himself with a woven black and white carpet. He lay on the dirt floor before a small corner fireplace where pinon logs were still smouldering.

Susan was the first to wake next morning. The sounds she heard were not the accustomed camp noises but a clatter in the *cocina* which joined their bedroom. She reached for her wrapper and roused the snoring Samuel with urgent shaking. "Someone's in the house! We're being robbed! In the kitchen!"

He grabbed his pistol and silenced Susan with a warning glance. Before he could investigate, however, a fat, kindly face, framed in smooth raven hair, peered from the doorway. *"Buenos dias, senor, senora. Chocolate ahora,* make chocoate now.'' She turned quickly with a swirl of skirt outlining her broad hips.

"Gracias,'' he mumbled, falling back sheepishly on the warm covers. "Mexican chocolate is the best in the world. I forget to tell you that James engaged a woman, Concha, to help in the kitchen – until you get used to being a housewife, that is.'' He playfully threw the covers over her head. "Take another 40 winks. She'll bring it in when it's ready. There'll be a houseboy too for running errands, keeping up the fires and such jobs. I'll leave the tent boys with the teams at the edge of town.''

"What about Jane?'' asked Susan, pinning back her thick dark hair.

"Oh, you can bring her here if you want or she can rest a while at the camp. Probably that would be best now.''

Susan propped up their pillows so they could drink the chocolate leisurely though she was eager to be up exploring her little casa on the Santa Fe River. One window of their bedroom opened to the north where she glimpsed the high peak of Santa Fe Baldy sprinkled with light snow that spilled down to the timberline. The other window in its deep recess of adobe wall framed a view of the church and the back side of the plaza. Dazzling sunlight poured in to reflect on the whitewashed wall where a small religious *santo* rested in its high niche above an all-purpose table. A mirror in Mexican tinware frame hung below the saint. One high back chair and a wooden bedstead with carved headboard completed the furnishings. As there was no covering on the chilly hardened-dirt floor, Susan was careful to pull on her shoes when she stepped out of bed. For the rest of their breakfast Concha had laid the table at the end of the main room though James still lay asleep before the fireplace. Like the bedroom, the walls of the front room were whitewashed and decorated with a length of calico extending halfway up the sides where wooden benches were placed for seating.

"That's a colorful piece of cloth,'' Susan commented, "but what purpose besides ornament does it serve?''

"To protect the clothing from whitewash when a person leans against the wall,'' replied Samuel. "I wouldn't be surprised if that goods hadn't come from our own wagons in a past season.''

The living room windows were deeply recessed, protected on the outside with turned wooden bars and secured on the inside with plank shutters which folded back against the wall. Susan thought the window ledge would serve nicely to store her books and maybe a plant, if she could have the houseboy dig up some native flower at the edge of town. The storage room on the north was dark and cool; it smelled of pinon logs, chili, melons and grapes which James had provided from the plaza stalls.

"Well, Mrs. Magoffin, how do you like your house?" asked her smiling husband as he rose from the table.

Susan threw her arms around him with an impulsive hug. "Such a question! You know I love it all. It's the first place where I could arrange my possessions along with yours. I'll fix it to suit the two of us and maybe we can invite some of your trader and army friends to visit."

"Don't worry, Pet, as soon as they find out where we are, they'll arrive in droves. And the socially prominent ladies of Santa Fe will also call, so keep yourself dressed and always have Concha serve a light refreshment. They're curious and gossipy but very friendly. Be prepared to try to respond in Spanish as best you can. And also, don't mention James and his mission in Santa Fe."

She was glad for the warning about James. It was hard to understand how it all happened according to a desperate and risky plan. She promised herself she'd forget the few details she knew. As for visitors, she thought that women everywhere were curious about newcomers, especially foreigners. It was no different here than in Kentucky and she admitted to herself that she was curious about them as well.

However, her first duty lay in giving instructions about their noon meal which James would share, a time at which she wanted to demonstrate her wifely skills to impress him. She need not have worried though, for Concha was already stewing mutton and preparing a baked dish of squash and onion. From out of the corner of her eye, Susan caught sight of a handful of red chili peppers going into the stew. "Oh, *poco, poco, no mas*, just a little, no more." she cried.

Concha looked up at her young mistress with a questioning smile. "*No pimienta, senora?*" She obediently picked out a few peppers with her long handled spoon, laying them aside for her own enjoyment.

Susan shook her head, fanned vigorously and blew little gusts of air from her mouth. Concha couldn't mistake her meaning and they both laughed at the success of her vivid, silent communication. "*Si, senora, si,*" Concha nodded in amused consent.

Susan knew at once that she had made her first friend in Santa Fe and she guessed that Concha could manage very well without her. She was further encouraged at lunch when James praised her for her stoic acceptance of trail hardships, calling her a philosophic little lady, one wise beyond her years, able to travel any place that fortune should lead them. She took the compliment from him gracefully but she watched her husband's reaction to their banter. Though he beamed proudly, she still felt guilty for causing him so much anxiety after the carriage accident and death of the baby. She promised herself that she would try even harder to live up to James' opinion of her, would be resolute and uncomplaining during the rest of their journey. She was beginning to think that Samuel himself needed to depend on her in difficult times and not always feel a slightly paternal responsibility. She wanted to be his partner, not his *pet*; she would ask him not to call her that any more, not even *querida*, the Spanish name for pet.

That very afternoon Susan's company began to arrive and she was glad that she was wearing Samuel's favorite dress for her first day's appearance as the pretty wife of a wealthy trader. The soft brown cashmere with its bodice fitted to her tiny waistline complimented highlights in her dark eyes and hair. A wide brown taffeta collar whose trimming of rose velvet ribbon brought out the color of her cheeks, fell softly over her breasts, corseted to a becoming fullness. She had scarcely finished her toilet before she heard Concha's steps at the door. From the woman's gasp of surprise Susan knew this was no ordinary visitor, and she too was taken aback when she recognized General Stephen Watts Kearny, Commander of the Army, and his aide Lucius Thruston. She extended her hand in her best Southern belle manner and was pleased that both gentlemen lightly kissed it in courtly fashion. "At your service, Madam," each murmured politely.

"General Kearny, you honor me by being my first American caller and I'm happy that a Kentuckian is also my guest," she exclaimed as she glanced up at the very tall Thruston. She was impressed by their contrasting height because Kearny was quite short, not much taller than she herself. "Please be seated, gentlemen. It's so nice to have you."

They occupied the *colchon* against the wall, Kearny sitting very erect in best military tradition. His clean shaven chin was held stiffly forward by the high gold embroidered collar of his uniform. Fringe on his shoulder epaulets showered sparks of light in the sun streaming from the window. Thruston wore no uniform as he was a civil appointee of the new government Kearny had proclaimed. Susan drew her straight chair a little nearer. Soon a subdued clatter of spoons and cups told her that Concha was preparing chocolate and bizcochitos.

Samuel returned unexpectedly to find the little group in animated conversation, the gentlemen feasting their eyes on the vivacious young hostess and Susan rising to the occasion. "Oh, *mi alma*, just see who's here," she exclaimed to her husband standing in the doorway. He took in the pleasant scene at a glance, beaming with pride at how well his Susanita was filling her new role as hostess.

"I was just telling your charming wife that I greatly regret the necessity of leaving so soon as my pleasure would be to remain in Santa Fe where I could call on her every afternoon," explained the General.

"Sire, since you've appointed me Prefect of Santa Fe, perhaps I can assume that delightful duty after our return from the lower villages,'' suggested Thruston. ''I'm sure the Magoffins and I have many friends in common back in Kentucky.''

''Oh, I'll be sure to come again before we proceed west to California,'' Kearny assured his hosts. He arose and bowed over Susan's little hand again. She notice the streaks of grey in his short black hair and the faint white line at his temples against sunburned skin that revealed a recent haircut. She knew that the General, also of Irish parentage like her husband, was only a few years older than he, but military life made him look more careworn and tired.

Susan didn't fare quite as well in entertaining Dona Juliana later that same afternoon. The friendly buxom matron let her darting eyes take in every detail of the house and its new mistress. Samuel was there to carry on the conversation in Spanish, but Susan generally understood the complimentary remarks the woman made about her – *''Buena nina, muy linda, muy afable* – good child, very pretty, very pleasing.''

After Dona Juliana had departed Susan said, ''Maybe she wanted to talk only to you, as I couldn't respond very well.''

Samuel smiled knowingly. ''I realize it is flattering for you to receive so much attention, Susanita, but guard your remarks. Here in Santa Fe the gossip grows with each retelling, the moral standards are quite different from those you've been taught and insatiable curiosity about newcomers will cause your callers to report every detail of your appearance, your house and certainly your conversation.''

''Oh, but I scarcely said a word this afternoon.''

''Yes, I know, and you need have no fear about Dona Juliana as she has been friends with the Magoffins for years, but I can't say as much for some of the other senoras. When they repeat domestic gossip about tales of infidelity, just smile and refuse to comment.''

Susan blinked at the word infidelity. ''You mean they actually talk about mistresses and –''

Samuel interrupted her with a laugh. ''Not only their husbands' mistresses, but their own current affairs, the *amante* of the moment. They may shock you, but they really mean no harm, for it's an accepted custom here for both husbands and wives to have affairs outside of marriage. The lower class can't afford the high fee charged by the clergy so they don't often bother with a formal marriage service. Divorce isn't permitted, but they continue to have affairs just the same. Their lack of private morals carries over into a very lax public morality as well.''

Next morning Susan saw Concha seating an early morning caller in the front room. It was the army doctor, Phillip Masure. I needn't be on guard with him, she thought. Since she was wearing a becoming wrapper purchased in New York, she didn't stop to finish dressing but hurried in to greet him. "Doctor, how pleasant to see you, how very nice of you to come." She extended both hands to him in affectionate welcome.

"Ah, Madame Magoffin, *bon jour, bon jour,*" exclaimed the little Frenchman, looking well groomed and handsome. His pressed uniform and neatly trimmed hair and beard were in great contrast to his tired, disheveled appearance at the Fort when Susan last saw him. "How well you are looking, exceptionally well, my dear."

"Thank you, Doctor. And I want to thank you again, more properly, I hope, for your care and attention to me at the Fort." Her eyes were brightened with sudden tears.

"Now, now, my dear, regret won't help, in fact it would be harmful to you in case you –"

"Do you mean that no permanent harm was done? That I'm still able to have a child provided that there is no accident this time?"

He looked down at her expectant young face, her slight, appealing little figure and smiled his reassurance. "I mean just that; your youth and natural good health should sustain you."

"I'm so relieved. I had worried so much for my husband's sake. Now you've made me very happy. Thank you, thank you for telling me."

"Right now I should also congratulate you for coming through Raton Pass without mishap to life and limb."

"That Pass is simply dreadful, isn't it? More hazardous to wagons and stock than the Jornada del Muerto they tell me."

The doctor rose and bowed courteously. "My dear, I'd like to talk longer, but I must get back to the Common where we are camping. Since I'll be marching with General Kearny tomorrow, I couldn't resist the opportunity of seeing you first. Give my warm regards to your husband." Masure kissed her hand again in true European fashion. From her window she waved goodbye, wondering if their paths would ever cross again, wondering what the future held for her in this strange but fascinating land.

She caught sight of herself in the mirror and smiled with satisfaction. Three separate gentlemen had kissed her hand, partly from custom, partly from genuine admiration. She was flattered at the attention. Does a proper married woman ever really desire the attention of other men, she asked herself? I'm certainly faithful to my husband, but why do I get flutters when men enter the room? Will I get over this feeling?

However, being mistress of her own little house, rented adobe that it was, gave her a womanly confidence she had never before experienced. She took great care that all should be in shining order when Samuel returned from his rented store in the plaza. But before she had finished, he arrived early, complaining of a headache and sore throat.

"Dearest, what causes this sudden illness? Do you have fever?"

"It's the dust; unpacking trail goods and setting up store is a dirty business. It's a common ailment. Some call it trader's disease, some the Santa Fe fever."

She looked so sad and concerned that he pinched her cheek playfully. "Don't worry, I'll be all right tomorrow. This fall weather will be making a glory of the aspen trees on the mountains in a few more days. The leaves are like tiny fans that quiver in the slightest breeze – quaking aspens, they're called. They're pretty enough in summer, but in late September and October they turn an unbelievable gold."

"I wish I could see them close up," she mused. "The cottonwoods along the alameda seem beautiful to me as they are showing gold in their leaves. I hope to remember enough about Santa Fe to write it all down, either in my journal or in letters back home. While you're resting, I think I'll begin a letter to Mama. I want to tell her about my illness at the Fort and losing –"

She had scarcely settled herself before a polite rapping announced another caller. Lt. Warner stood expectantly, military cap under his arm, when Susan opened the door. She couldn't conceal her surprise, particularly since he was alone. She wondered if he thought that she would be alone at this hour too. Her pulse quickened, showing a tell-tale pounding in her neck that was ill concealed by the loose collar of her housedress. There was something about the way he looked at her –

"Who is it?" called Samuel, attempting to rise from the *colchon* where he had been resting. He heard her say primly that her husband was ill. "Who is it?" he called.

Susan invited the Lieutenant into the living room thinking that now she had the two men together she might settle her feelings. She felt she must gain better control of herself as she couldn't always avoid him, at least until Kearny took his whole army on to claim California. That eager look in his eyes disturbed her. What was on his mind? What was on hers?

"Will you have tea or coffee?" she asked properly, gesturing toward a straight back chair, hoping he wouldn't be too comfortable or stay too long. Then she hastily went to the kitchen to speak to Concha, leaving the two men alone until the tray was ready.

The visit was stiff, conversation forced as Samuel's throat was too sore to talk much and she didn't know what to say herself. She was glad when Warner left. As he kissed her hand, which he hadn't done before, she drew it away quickly, wondering if Samuel noticed how it was shaking. Gratefully, she closed the door and returned to her letter writing.

63

The following days, routine as they were, passed happily for Susan. It was a relief to get up in the morning with the certain knowledge that there would be no unexpected danger, no misfortune to endure. She wished her mother and father could drop in to see how well she was managing in spite of their dire predictions that she was too young and too inexperienced for marriage and housekeeping. She was enjoying this placid interlude before the next stage of her adventure, their trip south to set up the store in Chihuahua – that is, provided James was successful in his second mission of U.S. intervention.

The variety of each day's visitors continued to surprise her. A gift of purple grapes came from the officers' camp and an Indian and a small Mexican market girl knocked on her door in the afternoon. She felt very important receiving the tall Indian chief who brought a letter addressed to General Kearny. She wondered why he had come to the Magoffin home to deliver it. Since she knew that all the northern tribes were sending representatives to deal with the new U.S. government in Santa Fe, she directed the chief to the officers' camp on the river. The chief looked upon her with utmost scrutiny.

Impressed as she was with the dignity of the man, it was Lupita, a diminutive *muchacha*, her basket loaded with squash, corn and green chili, who completely captured Susan's heart. "*Calabazas por real*, five cents," she chanted in a childish, singsong voice. She held a smooth, yellow sample for Susan's inspection, at the same time jiggling her basket so the fresh smell of green corn in husk and the enticing odor of slightly bruised chili pods would facilitate her sale.

"*Uno real! Demasiado mucho*, too much," said Susan, shaking her head. "*No tonta*, I'm not stupid."

Unabashed, the little girl tried another approach. "*Cuatro calabazas y un canto por real*, four squash and a song for five cents." She burst forth in a high thin soprano, singing an old folk tune for the *Americana* who weakened and began fishing in her pocket.

There after, the little girl appeared every morning with her basket until Susan began to depend on her for all their fresh produce. One day when a chill wind from the Sangre de Cristo range promised an early winter,Susan opened the door to find her *muchacha* shivering violently in her threadbare *manta*. She could scarcely hold her basket of dried beans. Susan put her arm around the girl and drew her into the front room by the fire. When the child put down the basket, Susan saw that her thin legs were blue with cold. All the pent-up maternal longing in her heart flowed out to the small girl who crouched by the fire. She called to Concha to bring a cup of hot chocolate.

Obediently the woman poked up the kitchen fire and noticed that

Susan seemed quite moved with pity. Concha jerked her head toward the child. *"Una bastarda, no buena."* She rubbed her fingers together in a gesture which surprised Susan.

"Oh, no, not that little one," she cried, eyeing the shivering child. "She seems too sweet to be dishonest. Surely she wouldn't steal from me."

Concha shrugged and began to pour the chocolate.

Susan kept the child in her warm room as long as she dared before Lupita left to finish her rounds. She had heard tales of heartless beating at home in the *barrio* if little beggars returned with their produce unsold. The grace with which the child moved and her polite manners made it hard for Susan to believe Concha's description, *una bastarda*. She began to toy with the idea that she might adopt the child and take her away from her hard life. If Concha were correct, the child was probably the offspring of an Anglo father and Mexican mother who might welcome one less mouth to feed. She resolved to talk to Samuel about it later. She needed a companion, especially since Jane had been neglectful of her duties lately. She took her sewing to the window while she waited for him.

Her husband, however, was not at all receptive to the idea of adoption. "She would be a great care for you, dear, not nearly as much help and company as you think."

"But she is so bright, so appealing She would learn to love us both and we would provide a better home than she could ever know."

"No, we must wait for our own child to love. I cannot agree to this plan under any condition." He walked over to look out toward the plaza where the last rays of the sun lighted the new flag. "Get your bonnet and shawl. I'll show you the Governor's Palace."

Susan felt that Samuel was treating her like a child, denying an important request, then pacifying her with a substitute pleasure. She had learned, however, not to press her point too far, but to try another approach at a later time.

The plaza looked much larger than it had the night of their arrival. It seemed darker too since there were no festive *luminarias* burning. Lamplight streamed through the front windows of the Palace onto a wide dirt walkway under the flat roofed portal. This same sheltered passage continued around the other three sides of the plaza. The Magoffins met a few other strolling couples who cast admiring glances in Susan's direction.

"Do you know them?" she whispered when Samuel greeted each with a cordial, *buenos noches.*

"Not all of them, but I recognize some as customers. I want them to notice the beautiful lady I'm escorting. See our store at the corner there, just across the plaza."

Because the shop was closed for the night, she couldn't see the stacked bales of clothing, yard goods, personal finery as well as hardware items that Samuel and his helpers had arranged for display. "I'm particularly anxious to have everything in readiness before invitations to the officers' ball are issued to the *gente fina*. Our sales should triple for that auspicious occasion."

"A ball? Where would it be held? Would we be invited?"

"You ask if the Magoffins would be invited? My dear, they wouldn't have it without us. Everyone is anxious to meet the beautiful Susanita."

"I'll be the only 'traderess' present." Susan's voice rose in excitement at mention of the ball. "Do you dance at the Mexican *bailes*, Samuel? I'd like to, very much. It's been a long, long time since I've dressed up and waltzed to good music."

"I don't really think you should count on dancing. I never learned how to dance, and it wouldn't be proper for a married woman unless she danced with her own husband, especially in Santa Fe where all eyes are watching."

"Oh, I hadn't thought about it that way."

"Sometimes these *bailes* get pretty lively, fast dancing, wild music, drinking. You'd be more comfortable on the sidelines, dear. You'll have all the attention you could possibly desire, especially from the officers." He squeezed her arm in reassurance. "You'll be the belle of the ball, whether you dance or not."

They walked the rest of the way home in silence, Susan pondering the new restrictions of her matronly status and the necessity for always conforming to someone else's preferences. I'm still young enough to crave excitement, she thought with a twinge of rebellion.

Next morning she was dismayed to find Lt. Warner again at her door. "I've come to invite you and your husband to the ball which the army is giving for all the traders who accompanied us on the trail. I beg the honor of a dance with you, Mrs. Magoffin, after you've danced with your husband first." He waited expectantly for her answer. His eyes caressed her until she felt herself blushing guiltily.

"Thank you for the invitation, Lieutenant. The Magoffins don't dance, but we'll be very glad to attend."

Her reply changed his flirtatious glance into a look of disappointment. "I'm so sorry, a waltz with you would have given me extreme pleasure, but I'm glad to know you'll be in attendance. The hour is set for nine o'clock at the large saloon on the plaza." He reached out to take her hand in farewell, his own moist palm trembling as he bent to kiss her delicate fingers.

Susan didn't return the amorous pressure but she felt lightheaded just the same. It annoyed her that her feelings were so easily aroused by the boyish, good-looking officer. She began to feel grateful for the stolid Samuel's preference for not dancing. If men near her own age gave her such flutters, perhaps it was good not to have the temptation of dancing with them.

The following night after an early supper, she began her preparations for the dance with a thorough brushing and coiling of her lovely dark hair. Jane had come in from the camp to assist in the intricate fastening and draping of her gown. "Miss Susan, I'm glad you're wearing gold satin tonight. The Mexican women wear so much red you'll stand out right smart and do Mr. Samuel proud with your good looks."

"Do you think so Jane? I've seen quite a few really beautiful *senoritas*. There's something about their flashing eyes that makes them irresistible."

"You're every bit as beautiful and your white skin makes you stand out in any crowd." Jane held the voluminous skirt so Susan could step into it. She adjusted the pillow-bustle and smoothed the black fringe which edged the rich drapery of the skirt and off-the-shoulder bodice. She handed Susan the gold satin, elbow-length gloves embroidered with jet beads and then closed all the tiny covered buttons. The settling of a black shawl, heavy with silk embroidery and fringe, over her mistress' slender shoulders completed Jane's duties.

Susan swept into the front room, swishing her skirts and taffeta petticoats as she curtsied low before her admiring husband. Little whiffs of French perfume rose when she unfurled her black silk fan.

"I'd rather stay here and feast my eyes on my Susan than go to any ball," he said. After a shadow of disappointment crossed Susan's radiant face, he hastened to make amends. "But I want others to appreciate your beauty too. Jane, tell Jose to finish blacking my boots. I mustn't keep the belle of the ball waiting."

After Samuel had given his wide silk tie a final tug, he put on his boots and declared himself ready. Jose waited in the Rockaway to drive them to the ball in high style.

All the young soldiers of General Kearny's command, under supervision of Lts. Warner and Hammond, had transformed the bare saloon into a ballroom of splendor – flags, bunting of red, white and blue hung on the walls and vigas. Susan coughed slightly as she breathed the smoky air which curled above the heads of the circling dancers. She was ushered to a seat beside the General himself.

Samuel leaned over to remove her shawl and whispered, "See, I told you that you would be the center of attention."

After a deferential wait for Samuel to dance with her, Major Swords came up and bowed low. "Madam, will you have a cigaritto?" He drew a small packet of corn shucks and a horn-shaped receptacle of coarse tobacco from his pocket, holding them out to Susan invitingly. The merry expression in his blue eyes showed her he considered the offer a joke, although his demeanor was quite proper before his commanding general. Samuel looked concerned lest his wife be offended and not understand the mischievous Major.

"Not this time, sir, thank you very kindly," she replied.

El Senor Vicario also advanced to pay his respects, his priestly robes swinging from side to side as he shifted his huge bulk through the crowd. Susan watched the dancers give way before him, choosing to break step in the reel rather than crash into such a formidable figure.

A quick flutter at the entrance became audible over the beat of jangling guitar and wail of violin. Again the crowd parted to let new arrivals pass, then just as quickly closed around them so Susan couldn't see who it was.

"La Tules, La Tules, herself!" whispered the shocked senoras seated along the wall near the door.

The soldiers turned to leer at the full-bosomed figure dressed in dramatic black velvet with a satin shawl of brilliant green that contrasted with her brightly-hennaed hair. They were no less surprised than the disapproving senoras when they recognized her escort as their officer, the respected Col. David Mitchell.

"Hmmm, something's afoot," murmured Samuel. "Dona Gertrudes Barcelo is the notorious monte dealer who runs the *sala* at the west end of Palace Avenue. Everyone knows her by sight or hearsay, except perhaps you, Susan. If she dares to approach the General, you must nod to her, but it won't be necessary to engage in conversation."

"I should hope not – that harlot has her nerve coming here, and with an officer at that."

Samuel nodded, then began to move down the hall toward the conspicuous late arrivals. He wished his brother were still in Santa Fe. James would certainly know if any intrigue involving Dona Tules were brewing.

Susan noted that Colonel Mitchell didn't seat Dona Tules with the rest of the senoras but stood uncertainly with her at the end of the room. She evidently wanted to dance for she began swaying her hips in time to the music and looked up at her escort invitingly from under lashes drooping with mascara. Taking the hint, he held out his arms and began to whirl her in a dizzying waltz.

General Kearny turned his attention to Susan. "Dona Tules' sala is the scene of frequent balls where the soldiers find entertainment. Unfortunately for them, they also leave most of their cash at her monte table. She's the shrewdest dealer of cards in the whole territory. It's rumored that she keeps an ox-hide chest full of gold and silver and wears the key around her neck."

Susan agreed with his description. Dona Tules did indeed look shrewd but flirtatious enough to lure many a homesick soldier to her hall of chance. She knew that the General would probably demand an explanation of his Colonel the next morning and thought it best to change the subject. "Why do some of the senoras use their servants as footstools? Isn't that a rather cruel and inhuman treatment?" She nodded toward several crouched figures across the hall who were patiently enduring the weight of heels on their backs.

"It is indeed a strange custom, but it keeps the drivers from getting into fights or drinking, as might happen in they remained outside with the carriages."

The sight moved Susan to pity. How strange are the customs of this foreign land, she thought, even if the inhabitants called themselves civilized. She also wondered if the garish costumes of the ladies were considered in good taste as each was weighted down with heavy jewelry, ribbons, bows and high combs. Her own gold satin dress seemed dull next to these overdone adornments. But the Spanish ladies certainly pleased their suitors, for as soon as a dance ended, they were rushed into another with a new partner. Susan wished she could dance with someone.

Next morning, an unexpected caller arrived at the Magoffin casa. Susan answered the door with the thought that her visitor probably was the persistent Lt. Warner wanting to know how she had enjoyed the ball. She was delighted, however, to see William, Samuel's younger brother, standing with his dusty trail hat tucked under his arm as he gave her a quick embrace.

"Will, oh, Will, we've been expecting you for the last two weeks!"

"Good morning, sister-in-law. The life of the wife must agree – you're prettier than when I last saw you in Independence. Is Sam around?" He walked into the bright front room, nodding approvingly at the furnishings.

"He went to his store on the Plaza. Where's Gabriel?"

"I left him at Raton Pass with the wagons. It was more than I could stand, all that breaking down and delay for repairs. I came ahead on horseback, thought maybe I'd help Sam with the store and maybe even entertain you."

"Since you left after we did, do you have any messages from home?

69

Any letter for me?'' Susan looked at him with a sudden longing for news of her family.

"There's a pretty good packet of them, some for Sam as well. I left them in my trunk in the wagon.''

"You left them? You mean you had letters for me which you didn't bother to bring with you? Oh, Will, how could you be so thoughtless?'' Her face flushed hotly with indignation.

"Calm down, girl, you'll get them. I didn't want to unpack my trunk. It was under all the extra supplies, too hard to reach.''

Susan crossed the room to look toward the mountains. God in heaven, give me patience with this young scamp, she whispered. She reached to pick up a book from the window shelf, replacing it quickly as she caught the embarrassed William grinning foolishly. "I think I've never heard such a lazy excuse, can you imagine how I've longed for news from home? You disgust me, really disgust me.''

William's amusement at her anger quickly changed with the realization that he might have taken the trouble to deliver her mail, entrusted to him in June, a full three months ago.

"I'd better find Sam, I don't seem welcome around here just now.'' His tall frame filled the low doorway as he stepped back into the sunshine of the September morning.

Without asking him to have coffee, Susan watched him untie his horse and ride to the plaza. Men, she thought, men *always* put their convenience before a woman's feelings. I'll punish him for this. But then Thruston appeared with military news that Mexican President, General Paredes, once a political exile in the United States and friendly with American officers, had been deposed. General Santa Ana had returned to power. With a sinking heart she realized that their troubles might be starting over again.

"We can only wait and see how this changeover will affect our cause,'' Thruston said.

The following day, Susan received a formal invitation to dinner from a Mrs. Leitensdorfer whom she had first seen at Bent's Fort. "You and your husband,'' the card read, "are requested to be our honored guests tomorrow at 2 o'clock.'' The General and his principal officers would be present. It would be a farewell party for the army.

Susan accepted the invitation, knowing she must make the best impression possible. Sometimes it seemed tiresome to be on display like a prize doll, but the unfailing compliments which she received made it easier to bear. She, in turn, was curious about a dinner in a well-to-do trader's home. Samuel had told her how that American merchants had influenced the economy and society of the ancient adobe city.

Next day when the Magoffins arrived, Susan was ushered to one of the cushioned benches on one side of the room while her husband sat with the men facing them. It was the same seating at the table, which placed her at a disadvantage to understand the significance of the discussion among the men which she preferred to the shrill chatter of the ladies. Therefore, she busied herself with tasting the two *sopas*, roasted meat and boiled meat stew, buttered rice with hard-boiled egg slices and a milk custard dessert which was lightened by beaten egg whites and delicate nutmeg seasoning. The dish, called *natillas*, reminded her of the custard pudding her mother made. Dr. Leitensdorfer's Missouri heritage had influenced his Spanish wife's cookery.

At the end of the meal, General Kearny raised his glass of champagne with a toast to "The United States of America and Mexico. They are now united, may no one ever think of separating." "*Viva, viva,*" Dr. Leitensdorfer responded. The remarks of both men were interpreted for the guests who didn't understand English. The dinner lasted nearly three hours and concluded when everyone except Susan smoked corn chuck cigarittos before departing.

The attentive little general, with fatherly interest in Susan's enjoyment of Santa Fe, escorted her to Catholic services the following Sunday. She noted in her journal that from her recessed seat in the vestibule, she could see little of the interior decoration.

Sunday, September 20th
Their music consisted of a violin, and a thumming jingling guitar;
the same tunes they had the night at the fandango. It is a strange
mode of worship to a Protestant who has been raised to regard the
Sabbath with strictest piety, not even to THINK of a dancing tune
on a violin, let alone the hearing of it.

She also commented to the General that she doubted the priest understood his mumbled Latin phrases any better than she, or the kneeling worshippers who crossed themselves frequently. Accustomed as she was to reading the Bible and religious books, she wondered how the unintelligible ceremony could help these people in their problems of daily life.

Since the visit to the church was somewhat disappointing, the kindly General insisted on a trip to Ft. Marcy, under construction on the top of a hill north of the village. They rode horseback through the tree-lined streets to inspect the artillery and the barracks which had first housed General Armijo's troops. They ascended the steep slope to view the valley spread out before them. "It's a perfect scene, as beautiful as the one at the summit of Raton Pass," Susan exclaimed. "I can count every house and building and see the crops on the plain beyond."

"Indeed," said the General, "this fort is a perfect defense for the seat of the United States government, and when the double adobe walls enclosing the military buildings and underground ammunition storage are complete, the place will be well nigh impregnable. I'm leaving Lieutenant Gilmer with his engineers to complete the place when I advance to California."

There was one more gala event to be crowded in before the troops departed. This time the newly appointed officials and citizen merchants were hosts to General Kearny and his entire corps in the ballroom of the ancient Governor's Palace. Susan was especially excited over the opportunity to see the interior of the historic place, the elaborately furnished rooms occupied by then-Governor Armijo, where James and Captain Cooke had conducted their secret meeting.

She arrived with Samuel when the tolling of church bells gave a signal that the ball had begun. A host of young officers who waited near the door for their arrival greeted them with enthusiasm. Lieutenant Warner hurried over to escort them to their seats, but Susan looked up at him, shook her head and took the proffered arm of a merchant who guided her to a special place. Samuel reached over to remove her brilliant red crepe shawl, deliberately chosen to compete with the vivid costumes of the Santa Fe ladies. "I think I'll just keep it on for a while," she whispered to him, "at least until everyone has had a good look at me."

This affair was no different from the first except for the improved surroundings. There was the same fast music, the same giddy, whirling dancers, the same thick smoke and dust. Susan wasn't as shocked this time when Dona Tules made her grand entrance with Colonel Mitchell. "I've never found out what the colonel is up to," Samuel whispered. "Word will leak out soon, I promise you."

Susan watched Tules and her partner swing into a native dance called the *Cuna* and tried to see whether a money box key or a crucifix was at the end of her heavy gold necklace. One couple at a time joined them until the floor gradually filled with swaying figures, arms encircling each other's waists while they leaned so far back that their hips and thighs were closely pressed together. The dancers resembled a human cradle, rocking back and forth, never losing step or altering the closeness of their unconventional position. Again she had to admit that Samuel was wise in declining to let her dance. What if an inebriated soldier or a drunken official had asked me to dance that dreadfully improper *Cuna*? What is Warner dared to claim me as a partner for *that* dance? She blushed furiously at the thought.

With the last violin notes of the farewell ball, the social scene in Santa Fe faded away. The next day the army prepared to march. Officers paid their hurried calls and Susan felt she might never see General Kearny again. Because of that sad realization, she treasured the happy visits she had enjoyed with him. In retrospect, even Lt. Warner was forgiven his flirtatious advances. She also thought that she would never again have so much flattering attention from so many men near her own age. In a way, she was whispering goodbye to her own girlhood.

In turn the soldiers wished the Magoffins a safe journey to Chihuahua as they followed the troops into their own equally uncertain destiny. Their last goodbyes, though voiced with optimism, held an unspoken note of sadness for them all.

The next week proved to be a dull one for Susan, especially since she was confined to her house to nurse the ailing Cousin Gabriel who had finally brought the wagons belonging to the Magoffin brothers safely through the Pass. While she administered to him her favorite remedy, Dr. Sappington's fever and ague pills, she had time to read and reread the letters which had at last been delivered into her eager hands.

The rumors and exaggerations that always accompany an army began to cause them more anxious concern with each passing day. The belief that the traders were in league with the Indians and the hated Texans against the Mexicans added to their fear. First they heard that General Taylor had been recalled from the south. Their own plans then became uncertain. Other news came that Colonel Mitchell with his "Chihuahua Regulars" had been ordered to join General Wool but lacked the government funds to reoutfit his men for the southern expedition.

Samuel came home one evening from repacking his remaining goods with a note of suppressed excitement in his voice. "I heard today the most amazing explanation of Dona Tules' appearance at the balls with Colonel Mitchell."

Susan looked up from her book. "Why, Samuel Magoffin, what do *you* know about Dona Tules, shameless harlot that she is?"

"Nothing personally, not a thing, not a thing...first hand," he assured her.

"Well, I should hope not! What did you hear?"

"The quartermaster in charge of supplies came to our store for some items of clothing and staples which he paid for in U.S. dollars. Since it's been fairly common knowledge among us merchants that the government was too hard pressed for cash to outfit Colonel Mitchell, we began to wonder where this American money came from. In fact, we ourselves had been paid with as many brass buttons cut from soldiers' uniforms as we could afford to accept in trade. Even the villagers refused to trade food for those blasted buttons. You remember that General Kearny gave orders that all supplies be paid for, not seized as contraband of war. Well, everyone is talking about the sudden appearance of hard cash. Do you recall Arturo and Romero, the men James brought to the carriage the night we arrived? They overheard joking remarks about Dona Tules being the only person in Santa Fe who had surplus funds. From what they said, we figured that she must have hoarded all the money the soldiers lost at her gaming tables.''

''But why would she want to loan money to an army which had overthrown her own government?'' Susan asked.

''A woman scorned, my dear,'' he answered.

''I don't understand.''

''It's a delicate situation to discuss, Susanita, but Dona Tules at one time had been Governor Armijo's favorite mistress until he jilted her for a younger woman. Tules must have felt she was getting even with him by outfitting his enemy and preventing his return to Santa Fe.''

Susan flashed a smile of understanding, ''In that case, I don't blame her. It was a glorious revenge, wasn't it?''

''It was more than that. Tules was trying to make her own position in Santa Fe society more respectable by appearing at balls where General Kearny was host and honored guest. With a military governor occupying the Palace, she improved her chances for official condonement of her establishment by the loan of $1,000 U.S. dollars. That's why Colonel Mitchell sealed the bargain by escorting her to the balls.''

''One thousand dollars? That's an awful lot of money. Will she be repaid?''

''Not any time soon, unless she can use a trunkful of brass buttons. The officers themselves haven't been paid wages in weeks, and the enlisted men are on short rations wearing tattered uniforms.''

''Did any government cash go to buy off Governor Armijo?''

''That we'll never know. James wouldn't discuss it with me.'' Samuel suddenly changed the subject. ''If I were you, I'd start packing tomorrow. When the soldiers are ready, we'll have to leave on very short notice, very short indeed.''

With the Kearny forces gone, Susan's days became an indifferent round of duties in her first house which she would soon leave forever. Her little market girl Lupita didn't even come, and in a way Susan was glad. She couldn't endure a tearful farewell with the child who was now so dear to her, in spite of Concha's warning. She felt a familiar stab of worry over news of another Indian uprising along the route they must follow. Governor Armijo's forces, said to be rearming and assembling for a return to Santa Fe, posed an added threat.

She spent part of the last night in her little casa watching the moon rise behind the Sangre de Cristo peaks. Silently she prayed that their future, now dark as the shadows in the mountain, would grow brighter.

7

The Magoffins started south on October 7th on the second half of their perilous journey. All three sections of their wagon train were now joined for protection, as William and Gabriel Valdez were riding to Chihuahua, Mexico with them. Since the Kearny forces had left only a small garrison in Santa Fe when the general headed west, it was as dangerous to remain there and face growing Mexican resentment as it was to follow the army farther into enemy territory. It was a desperate choice, but traders were accustomed to taking such chances. Samuel hoped, however, that James' second mission of persuading Mexican officials not to resist the Army's advance would assure them of a fairly safe passage. But that, too, was a desperate hope.

When they were a few days out, a scout brought disturbing news. Riding hard to meet the wagon train, he told how Apaches had robbed James and his driver Jose Gonzales of their carriage, mules, trunks and cash. Either they were left to die in the desert or were taken as captives to a camp in the foothills. Samuel drew a deep breath and cast an anxious glance toward Susan.

"Did the Indians *scalp* my brother? Was any trace of him found?" Samuel asked out of earshot of his wife.

"No, senor, all we found were their big hats caught on a thorn under the mesquite bushes. There was no sign of blood."

"No sign of violence at all?" Samuel wiped his damp forehead with a crumpled handkerchief. "Did you find any tracks leading away?"

"There were lots of moccasin prints around the wheel marks but none we could trace very far. We followed the trail of the carriage for some distance but we saw nothing of the white men or any of their possessions. We figure your brother and Gonzales were resting from the noon heat. They heard the hoof beats thundering and had just enough time to crawl back to hide in the thick mesquite bushes. They let the Indians take the mules and carriage in order to save their own scalps."

"That's probably what happened. Yes, it must have been that way. Apaches usually don't let captives off easily." Then he gave orders to double the guards around the wagons. There was no use keeping the facts from Susan, so he explained them to her. "Do you still have your pistol handy? Perhaps we'd better have some target practice when we get away from the villages."

She paled at his words. "I hope it's all rumor! Poor Jim, what a terrible fate. And what about us? Without him to negotiate with the Mexican general what will the traders do?"

"Let's hope this set-back won't stop him. He's lived through other dangers. If he's still alive, I'll wager that he's on his way to Mexico."

The wagon train, following the troops, continued its dragging pace down the Rio Grande through deep sand toward the small village of Albuquerque. They had passed the "table plains" or mesas and camped across the river from a peaceful village whose Indian inhabitants brought eggs, chickens and fruit to trade for goods. Susan had become more tolerant of staring eyes. She allowed women to finger the cloth of her dress and shawl, laughing with them when they discovered that she wore high-laced shoes instead of moccasins.

"They are surprised that I have the same number of arms and legs as they do," she commented to Samuel.

Before the Magoffin wagons were ready to break camp next day, a group of eager squaws arrived with baskets piled high with fall apples, onions and watermelons. They wanted to trade their produce for the empty wine bottles which Samuel saved. Susan was surprised at how the black bottles seemed so favored. "What will they do with old bottles?" she asked. "This woman here has offered me five melons for that black medicine bottle."

"They make wine from their grapes, dark bottles keep it better. The Spanish padres who brought vines up from Mexico taught the native farmers how to cultivate vineyards and bottle wine. Charge at least fifty cents a bottle, he cautioned, turning away to check a big basket of assorted fruit.

"Why, that's $6.00 a dozen just for the empties which we bought full for only $3.00 a dozen back home!" she exclaimed.

Samuel, shrewd trader that he was, shrugged, "We've already lost money due to forced trade with the army and their brass buttons instead of cash. We have to make up the difference the best way we can."

The old *comadre* had stood patiently by the wagon while Susan talked to her husband. Her eyes never left the shiny black bottle. The woman stooped quickly, reached into a woven basket and held out a corn shuck package of fresh tortillas and at the same time pointed again to the five melons in her willow hamper. Susan handed her the bottle and added a small brown one.

"*Gracias, muchas gracias.*"

"What a kind, sweet face she has." Susan said.

"Her years have brought her wisdom; she's a better trader than you."

"What do you mean?"

"The brown bottle, being square, was worth more than the black one and tortillas aren't equal to melons." Samuel grinned with good nature at Susan's short-sided trade.

It was such amusing details of every-day living that occupied Susan's mind and kept her from thinking about uncertainty. In a land of isolation, they nevertheless continued to receive news by army courier. General Kearny was said to have been met by Kit Carson with word that California territory was taken over by Commodore Stockton and the Pacific Fleet. Kearny sent his men back to New Mexico and proceeded west with only a very small guard of 100 dragoons to meet the Commodore and secure the interior of the far western province. This was cheering news indeed. It raised hopes for a similar takeover of Chihuahua – if Jim had escaped with his life and could carry out his secret mission, all would be well.

While they were camped to rest the animals before starting through the waterless desert called the *Jornado del Muerto*, Journey of the Dead, Susan spent her idle time sewing a dress of thin cotton. She hoped to have the long, tedious seams of the skirt finished before they reached the warm regions below the Rio Grande. One afternoon she was joined by another *comadre* from the pueblo who watched closely as Susan's nimble fingers stitched away at the dress. As usual, she answered personal questions about her family in Kentucky, her husband, how he was much older than she. The woman asked why she had run off with him from her childhood home to live in a wagon along the trail. Susan explained she loved Samuel and wanted to be with him, wherever he went. The woman looked at her steadily before she replied, "*Si, el marido es todo del mundo a las mujeres* – the husband is the whole world to women."

Susan nodded in agreement and thought, as she had many times before, that these native women, in their simple wisdom, were like all women the world over.

This brief interlude of rest was interrupted by an urgent messenger from the trader camp 30 miles down river. Mexican spies, captured that very morning, had confirmed the previous rumor that a large force was marching up from Chihuahua. After delivering this message, the courier started on to Santa Fe to urge Doniphan's troops to make all possible haste to join the trader's wagons. Captain Hall and other trail-masters gave orders that each night the wagons should be corraled in a defensive circle with their wheels buried up to the hubs in sand in order to form a firing breastwork. Since the North Pass at El Paso was blockaded by Mexican troops, the Americans would be forced to wait in the desert – perhaps to face a worse test under the scorching sun.

Susan's fearful thoughts were interrupted by a child.

"*Donde esta el Senor Magoffin?*" a small boy said.

Samuel came forward to meet a thin boy, nine or ten, picking his way barefoot through the cactus.

"*El Senor Magoffin! Me llama Francisco.* My name is Francisco. The old man across the river sent me here. He wants you to buy me."

"Do what?" asked Samuel.

"*Por favor, senor,* please to buy me," the child repeated.

"Come inside, *muchacho*, let's have some breakfast before we strike a bargain." Samuel laid a hand on the bony little shoulder and gently guided the timid boy into the tent. Jane was serving plates with hot biscuit, bacon and molasses, and the tantalizing odor brought a quiver of excitement to the underfed child. He rubbed his mouth and licked thin lips.

"Jane, fill an extra plate; we have company for breakfast." He watched as the boy inhaled his food. "Now what is this about buying you?"

The boy hesitated, dropped his eyes before Susan's gaze.

"Who is the old man who sent you?"

"*Mi madre es muerto,*" the boy closed his eyes and folded his hands over his chest in a posture of death. "*Mi padre es muerto – Indios.*" He made a gesture of scalping around his forehead and jerked at a tuft of touseled black hair.

Susan shuddered, "*Pobrecito, pobrecito,*"

"What happened to you then?" Samuel asked, and the boy wrung out a halting story of slavery and privation. He told them that he was one of a group of children captured to serve an Apache chief and his squaw. The boys performed camp tasks, eating what was left from a common pot. Over the course of three long years, Francisco planned to escape, waiting for his chance. One day when they were sent to the river for water, Francisco and another boy caught a floating log and pushed off into midstream. The other boy did not conceal himself and was caught by a vigilant squaw. He never saw him again.

Francisco told how he paddled his way down river until he found a small hut near the bank where the old man sat shelling beans in the sunshine. He climbed the muddy slope and ran to throw himself at the *compadre's* feet. Half in Spanish, half in Apache, he told his story. The man divided his meager food, but it was not enough, so when Francisco saw traders camped near the adobe hut, he headed in that direction.

"Why did you ask me to buy you?" Samuel asked.

"Senor Torres, he spend pesos for food. He say I no worth that much. He say you can have me for seven dollars." He held up seven brown fingers to show the total sum.

"You stay here with Susanita. I'll go bargain with Torres."

And thus it happened that the unfortunate child became the object of Susan's affection. Francisco squatted down by the tent pole which he grasped with his dirty hand, and his sorrowful eyes followed her as she reached into her hide trunk for a light shawl. Though he acted afraid of her, his whole being responded to a woman's voice.

She stepped outside the tent and called, "Jose, Comapu, *aqui, pronto!*" Comapu arose, stuck out his lower lip in typical native fashion to indicate the direction of his summons. Then he turned to beckon vigorously to lazy Jose still stretched by the fire. Ever since the carriage accident Comapu had been quick to answer Susan's bidding as if by his eager actions he could reverse the sorrow he had caused her.

"*Vengo, senora,* I come."

Susan pulled back the tent flap and motioned him inside. Comapu stared at the frightened boy who sat with his head bent over his knees as if to ward off an expected blow. Susan explained that the child's name was Francisco. "Bathe him, cut his shaggy hair and find him a clean shirt and jacket. If it's too long in the sleeves or tail, bring it back and I'll cut it down. I want you to take charge of him for me, place a blanket for him beside yours tonight and see that he has all he wants to eat."

"Si, senora," answered the Indian driver. He grasped the child's shoulder and half pulled him to his feet. "*Vamos.*"

The next day she called Francisco to bring Ring and walk with her down toward the river. It was a bright October day when the chill of the morning had given way to pleasant, comforting warmth, so unlike the burning heat of summer. A few persistent cicadas whirred in the mesquite branches in a last mating call before the frost of cold nights ended their brief lives. Ring bounded crazily beside the boy, catching sticks Francisco threw for him, barking and scrambling noisily over the rocky soil. Suddenly the child froze in his steps, head cocked to one side. His eyes searched the ground where Susan was walking and humming a light tune to herself.

"*Senora, serpiente! serpiente!*" He made a gliding motion back and forth with his hand while his eyes never left the ground. Ring came running back to sniff around the cactus, backed off and growled low in his throat.

Because of the insect whirr and the distracting antics of the dog, Susan hadn't heard the warning rattle of death. She gathered her skirts tightly around her ankles, not daring to move as the unmistakable rattle threatened again and again. Francisco stooped calmly, picked up a sizable rock and with precise aim smashed the snake's head. The sinuous body thrashed wildly in the brush. Now she saw that she had been walking directly into its path and would have been struck without Francisco's warning. She gave him a sudden hug of appreciation.

The child looked at her intently. Then a boyish grin spread over his bony face. Whistling to Ring, he ran toward the river.

Food and security soon gave Francisco back to himself. In the evenings around the fire he sat entranced while Comapu strummed his rawhide guitar. He never joined the singing but he beat the ground with a stick, Indian-drum fashion.

The black men in the train and Jane, her head bound neatly in a white kerchief, puzzled him. He stared curiously each time he was near them. "Did the *hombres* sleep in the sun too long? What makes them black?" he asked Comapu.

"The Great Spirit makes different colors," Comapu answered.

Francisco accepted this simple explanation. If the Great Spirit planned them that way it must be right. In his childish innocence he believed all earth people were the same. Sometimes they became wicked when the Evil Eye hexed them. Otherwise all men were brothers.

Susan was the first of the Magoffins to succumb to trail fever. She was confined to her bed in the tent which, from months of pitching and unpitching, was tearing at its canvas sides. The roof had been mended countless times. The floor was worn thin by constant treading on rocky ground. The cold crept under the flaps at night. Susan called her illness a light fever, but it was aggravated by malaria contracted from camping near mosquito-infested river bottoms during the summer. She was miserable, listless, scarcely answering Samuel's questions.

"Tell Jane to bring a cup of tea, not coffee," she said, "and hand me the box of Dr. Sappington's pills as they surely help my aching bones – at least for a little while."

Francisco and Ring arrived to keep vigil beside her bed. The child's wide, solemn eyes never left her face except when he corrected Ring to keep the dog's scratching and tail-thumping from rousing Susan from her uneasy, tossing sleep. Perhaps the boy had also watched beside his own mother as she lay dying. Perhaps the fear in his eyes came from sadness that this kind senora might also be taken from him.

By the third day Susan's throat was so swollen she could not swallow hot tea, coughing racked her frail body so that it was hard for her to stay covered. Samuel pursed his lips into a firm line of decision and called Jane. "Pack her gowns and extra clean bedding and covers. I'm going to Valverde to find better shelter than this drafty tent." He returned just before sundown and hitched up the Dearborn carriage which Jane had made down into the bed. It seemed years ago instead of only a few months since he had loaded her into the same carriage at Bent's Fort. He gathered bread, tea, coffee, some dried fruit from the wagon stores and tucked it into a box by the driver's seat.

In Valverde, he located an adobe dwelling, simple in furnishings but with a tight roof and windows. Also there was ample firewood stacked outside. Samuel asked that a narrow couch be moved into the room with a corner fireplace. He placed two sheep wool mattresses upon it for extra warmth and comfort.

His own blanket was thrown on the floor beside her bed so that he could keep a steady fire roaring all night.

However, in spite of his diligent care, she was worse the next morning. He summoned Jane from the kitchen to watch. "I'm going to send for the camp physician down river," he said. "Surely the army can spare him for a few hours."

"Yass sir," Jane replied. "I won't stir from this place, I'll watch every move she makes."

When Samuel returned with Dr. Simpson and his black bag lined with pill bottles, Jane opened the door for them, put a finger on her lips and shook her head sadly. "Mr. Samuel, she's been talkin' all day, out of her head, she is, thinks she's back home, keeps callin' her mama to bring her a drink of spring water. I put cold cloths on her head, but she still keeps talkin' crazy like."

The doctor listened to her rasping breath. "I'll do what I can, sir, but she should certainly have received medical attention before now."

"I know, I know, but she didn't want to leave camp even yesterday morning when she was too sick to raise her head from the pillow. Tell me what to do, Doctor."

There was not much that could be done. Like countless people who had suffered trail fever before her, Susan's recovery lay in her own physical stamina. When one of their number was ailing, the traders sometimes laughed at their predicament. "You either die or get well out on this prairie," one of them said to Samuel. Another added, "By the time a doctor can reach a patient, riding miles on horseback or in a buckboard, a baby is usually three or four days old. Where I come from the stork beats the doctor."

Samuel and Jane sat by the sick bed day and night. He prayed aloud that her youthful endurance would overcome the ravages of fever. Susan managed to swallow the various pills and remedies left by the doctor until at the end of a week the fever broke.

She gradually ceased shivering. The fireplace brought cheer to her tiny room. Samuel told Jane to, "make a mutton broth and feed her with a spoon. Don't press too much on her at once but offer very frequently. I'm going to find goat's milk in the village and maybe some eggs. I give thanks to the Good Lord for His care so that perhaps she'll take a little nourishment and grow stronger."

Another full week passed in the rented adobe before Susan could sit up in bed and look through a small, ising-glass window set into the thick wall. They were less than 200 miles from Santa Fe, but it seemed the safety of Fort Marcy was a dream of great distance, many years away. It was necessary for Samuel to go back to the wagon camp regularly for the news that was daily expected from the Pass. Through all of Susan's illness, he waited the dreaded word that Mexican forces might cut them off in both directions, and that they might be annihilated before Colonel Doniphan returned from his expedition to the Navajo country.

He kept his worries to himself, however, and devoted all the time he could spare to keeping Susan cheerful. On the afternoon of November 18 she felt well enough to sit by the fire to make an entry in her journal.

Wednesday, November 18

This is the first day I have dined at table in two whole weeks. I have had a letter from home, yes, all the way from Lexington, dated September 10. It makes me long to be there. But I won't be impatient, if we live, the time is coming for us to be together again.

The owner of the adobe and his wife brought a dessert of bread and raisins with cinnamon flavoring. They entertained her with stories of the feast days of the patron saint, San Gabriel, of the village.

Later she watched from the window the celebration when a statue of the saint was carried around the plaza by priests and others bearing the cross and religious symbols. Little pitch fires lighted the route of the procession. Smoke streamed over the marchers; she could even smell it in the casa. The music of violins, drums and a metallic sound that must have been a triangle beat with a drum stick. The people marched around the plaza until it was time for the Fiesta ball. Later every one entered the hall on the plaza, the little fires finally burned out, and Samuel helped her back to bed.

She lay contentedly watching the flames in the corner fireplace cast dancing shadows on the hand-plastered wall. She knew with certainty that her faithful husband would keep the logs burning for her continued comfort. Dear, steady Samuel. She now had come to accept his trader's way of life, to know that love is not measured by constant attention and fancy words, that his presence when really necessary showed her the true extent of his devotion.

The Magoffins enjoyed little more than a week of domestic tranquility. Disturbing news of the war and brother James came on December 1. Susan sensed immediately that something terrible had happened. "Tell me what it is, Samuel, I have a right to know."

He smoothed her hair and drew her to him for comfort. "We've had direct word that Jim is in prison; he will stand trial for his life as a spy against the Mexican government."

"A spy? His intentions weren't to spy, only to keep the peace between two governments."

"I know, that's our side of the question. The letter from President Polk introducing James to General Wool, like a similar one to Kearny, has been seized by a soldier and the evidence against James is overwhelming. You remember Dr. Connelly and Frank McManus started out with Jim from Santa Fe and that they really managed to escape from the Apaches?"

"I remember. It was dreadful then and still is. I've been afraid for his life ever since."

Samuel continued to explain. "I hoped that first they would make their way to El Paso to negotiate terms for our wagons to enter. Then Jim would proceed to Chihuahua. But since this incriminating letter has entered the picture, his future really looks dark indeed."

"What will happen?"

"There's no way of knowing."

Susan clasped her hands. "How could we have known that this trip would turn out to be so disastrous for us all?"

"Everything in life is a risk, Susanita. Sometimes things are worse than we expect." He didn't tell her at this time that General Zachary Taylor had lost 1,000 of his men in a severe battle near Monterrey, deep in Old Mexico near the mouth of the Rio Grande. It would be too hard for her to understand the complexity of army maneuvers, the conflicting daily reports filtering in. By the time the traders received military news, circumstances had changed, uncertainties grown worse.

By Sunday, December 6, the situation worsened and Samuel suggested they keep their possessions ready to move on short notice.

"Have you had any further word from Jim?" she asked when he mentioned that Taylor was preparing for an active fight with Santa Ana's forces.

"None at all. He may languish in that Mexican prison indefinitely before his trial comes up. If Santa Ana loses, James may stand a chance but if our American troops are defeated and Taylor makes another military mistake, Mexican officials may put him to death without a hearing."

"It's all so confusing," she complained to Samuel when he told her this latest development. "The army keeps changing plans. What can we count on?"

"It is confusing, but it would be very rash for us to leave here until we have more positive news that Wool is actually on his way to join us. I know that arid country well, and its people. We could be rushing into a veritable death trap. I can't convince the hotheads in the wagon camp though. They're tired of waiting. They want action, but I will absolutely not leave unless the news is better. I would rather start our wagons back to Fort Marcy alone, if need be."

Trouble on her own domestic front also added to Susan's personal worries. Jane had been extremely indifferent to Susan ever since she recovered from the fever. She was cross, even rebellious at extra work. She refused to do all the cooking, leaving her mistress to prepare the meals alone. Susan tried to excuse Jane's insolence on grounds that the woman was terribly homesick. She resolved not to bother her husband with these troubles, for Samuel seemed more distressed than usual. He was having a difficult time keeping the wagon camp from rebelling and the drivers rushing south to war.

Their trader friends, Col. Owens and Edward Glasgow, called at the casa to say that they were on the way to El Paso, notwithstanding the danger they might be rushing into. Indeed, it was hard to maintain the camp because of the need for new grazing grounds for the livestock. These men, steady going merchants as they were, nevertheless had made the decision to go on without the army. They reduced their train by repacking and sending back a few empty wagons to Missouri.

Early next morning Susan waited in vain for Jane to clear the kitchen and help with the tasks. About 10 o'clock, Francisco, Ring at his heels, rapped on her door to deliver a message. "Senora Magoffin, *su criada* wants me to tell you she leaving with black man and Captain Owen's wagons. She go back home. She want no more wagon train. She scared of Mexicans. She say she will tell your padre you all right."

She motioned the boy to wait beside the fire and stepped into the adjacent storage room. When she closed the door, she leaned limply against the wall, tears streaming down her pallid cheeks. "Jane, my faithful Jane, gone home and I'm still here in this awful, terrible place! How could she, oh, how could she? She knows how much I need her! I can't stand it without her help, I can't. I can't. I can't."

84

She lifted her apron to wipe away the tears and felt the stiff envelope of her last letter from home folded in the pocket. Her fingers closed over it, a desperate clinging to her vanishing security. How could she tell Samuel? She could imagine the heat of his indignation. But how could she be angry at Jane? Secretly she was glad the black teamster would take her to safety.

On the morning of December 19, a scout said: "There are 700 regulars already at the Pass and 3,000 more marching up from Chihuahua. They have captured several hundred Americans."

"That must be Major Gilpin's company," Samuel reflected when he heard the man's hysterical report.

"There were only 900 of our troops to begin with," replied Captain Hall. "They would be well nigh cut to pieces by superior Mexican forces, if this were true."

That night Samuel couldn't eat supper. He walked the floor, no longer concealing his anxiety. "It is best you know, Susan, my dear, that our situation is desperate."

"I'm not afraid as long as you are with me," she said bravely, "but it's hard to bear the thought of your being put in prison or – or my being manhandled by..." She buried her face in her hands, shoulders shaking with her sobs.

Samuel reached over to hold her close.

Two days before Christmas they heard that the American forces had united at last under Generals Wool and Taylor, and that they were finally advancing on the Mexican Commander Santa Ana. They passed the holiday in an almost futile hope that the U.S. army would triumph. That was their Christmas celebration.

There was nothing to do in the little casa except wait and wait and wait.

Susan took up her diary, concluding with thoughts of her pioneer grandmother.

Tuesday, December 29th

These are truly exciting times! I doubt if my honored grandmother ever saw or heard more to excite in the War of 1812 than I have here. Indians are all around us, coming into the soldiers' camp and driving off their livestock, killing the men in attendance.

She thought that perhaps she could tell her granddaughter about her troubles – if she lived to have a granddaughter. Jealousy, suspicion, thoughts of death were very poor company for a girl as young as Susan — whose trials were far from over.

8

Christmas morning in Colonel Doniphan's camp dawned under the Organ Mountains in southern New Mexico, named because their rugged summits looked like a row of church organ pipes. The small force of about 800 men were slow to begin their usual tasks gathering wood, rounding stock. Younger volunteers, remembering their Missouri heritage, shouted a few snatches of holiday songs as they worked.

While back home family and friends were opening presents and singing carols, Doniphan's troops, with a strong front and rear guard, began their short march. The flat land was studded with chaparral and mesquite and the men missed the tall evergreens of home. The Pass was about 30 miles away where they knew they would meet the enemy.

Lt. James Lea had been dispatched to bring a cannon down from Fort Marcy before the battle at the Pass. "We camped at Brazito," he wrote, "the little side arm of the Rio Grande, in clear view of the mountains and all the surrounding country. Colonel Doniphan marched only 18 miles that morning and pitched camp early, it being Christmas Day. While the men were gathering sage and mesquite roots for the evening fires, the Colonel and a few officers spread out cards on a blanket to play three-trick lou. A handsome stallion had been rounded up with captured Mexican horses the day before and the officers were playing with the horse as a stake.

"Doniphan had just drawn a winning card when he glanced up to see a rising dust cloud. It was the advance guard riding back to camp, shouting, 'Enemy advancing! Enemy upon us!' The Colonel threw down that good card, called to the bugler and jumped on his horse. He circled the camp, marshalling the scattered troops under the nearest standard. They dropped their wood and buckets and ran like hell. In no time most of the company was in battle station awaiting the command to fire. In the distance the Mexicans could be seen, maybe a thousand or more.

"General Ponce de Leon himself marched with them. I never saw such grand uniforms as they wore – blue pants, green coats with scarlet braid, and tall caps with a waving plume of horse-tail. Their swords and lances glittered like all get-out in the bright noon sun.

"Colonel Doniphan sat his horse in front of his men as cool as you please. A messenger, waving a black flag with white skull and cross-bones on it, darted from the Mexican ranks and stopped about 50 yards away from him. The Colonel made a sign to his interpreter who advanced a ways and waited. We heard a man yell something in Spanish. The interpreter said he was calling for our commander to appear before the Mexican General. So this here interpreter called back, 'If your general wants peace, let him come here first.' That messenger said nothing else, just kept waving that flag around until we could see the opposite side was lettered, *Libertad O Muerte.*

"Then the Mexican wheeled his horse, calling over his shoulder, 'Prepare for charge, no quarter asked, no quarter given!'

"A great peal of the trumpet signaled an enemy charge to our left. The men held their fire until the Mexicans were at close range. They had fallen flat in the underbrush at Doniphan's command 'Squat.' They didn't even raise their heads when the enemy balls began to whistle over them. This took those dandies by surprise as they couldn't judge their aim. Just about that time Captain Reid with a few mounted men broke through the Mexican troops and began hacking around with their sabres. Those who escaped raced to attack the commissary and baggage wagons. Our men were ready for them, though. They were protected by the wagon canvas and fired only when sure of deadly aim. Our boys held fire, squatting low behind the chaparral as Doniphan commanded until the Mexicans were practically walking on them. Then the first row of men opened fire, followed quickly by the second while the first bunch reloaded. The Mexicans were surprised to see men popping up from behind all those bushes. They thought that those standing up were trying to surrender. They came in real fast, calling, *'bueno, bueno,* til they were close enough for our whole right wing to fire at once. You should have seen them run! When the men in the rear saw the front line waver and crumble, the whole bunch turned back, those that were able to run, that is. Nearly 50 were killed outright, three times as many fell wounded.

"Our horsemen chased them at least a mile but since the whole bunch had turned tail to hide in the foothills, Doniphan didn't pursue them farther as it would be dangerous in losing his men and it was getting dark. He knew that he couldn't successfully engage them again at the Pass without heavy artillery. He wisely waited.

"On our side only eight wounded, none killed. You should have seen those Missouri boys showing off their wounds, proud as Christmas presents. It was the first engagement since enlistment, six months of waiting. A fine celebration for those boys, all right. Next morning we tended to their wounded prisoners and sent them back to the Pass. The rest we buried."

Susan noted the event in her diary.

Some days after Lt. Lea's written dispatch of the battle, a scout reported that Doniphan had reached the Pass to enter the town of El Paso on December 29. The Mexican army evacuated the day before. Doniphan was surprised to have Mexican citizens wave white flags on the outskirts of the village. They offered to surrender, if he would show clemency in sparing their lives and property. This development was as unexpected to Doniphan as the lack of resistance had been to Kearny in August. In both cases, Mexican forces fled before the U.S. advance.

The scout described how the Colonel assured the terrified inhabitants that he had not come to plunder but to offer them liberty and peace. Like Kearny, he also warned them that punishment would be meted out to all who took up arms against the Americans. He promised to purchase all supplies for his men and animals and pay a just price. He also promised that the settlement would not be destroyed or harmed in any way.

While this news was reassuring to Susan, she was too tired to spend much time rejoicing over military victory. Little Francisco was ill. Susan's heart ached for the child who was unable to describe what ailed him. His misery, coupled with fear, was hard for her to watch.

He remained distant and cowering.

"No remedio, senora, no remedio," he protested when she tried to give him fever pills, his eyes dilating in terror at the sight of the big blue capsules. Since he refused the capsules, Susan poured tonic into a spoon and held it to his lips. He promptly spit it out. She despaired of helping him except by giving nourishing broth and keeping him warm by the fire. She tried to calm his fears by smoothing his hair, but he flinched at her touch. Perhaps he thought he was being punished with the bad medicine she offered.

It was now mid-January 1847. The whole village was ill with infections of nose and throat. Sanitation and personal hygiene were not the universal practice. Word had spread that the merchant Magoffin could cure ailments and aches miraculously. Susan examined so many patients that she came down with a severe cold that required strong onion poultices and night sweating to relieve. "Francisco and I can watch over each other," she explained to Samuel. "I just don't believe I can face another sick person until I feel better myself."

The bleak landscape and the cold depressed Susan's spirits. Her depression was deepened by the ugly news that Lt. James Lea brought back from his hurried trip to the capital city. He reported that Colonel Sterling Price, by then hated and feared, had been forced to arrest the leaders of an uprising against the Americans. "Diego Archuleta, Tomas Ortiz and Captain Salazar were their names," Lea reported. "These men had succeeded in arousing the natives, both New Mexican and Indian against the Americans in a scheme to overthrow their conquerors. Since the Pueblo Indians were also disillusioned by the pale faces from the east, they joined forces with the New Mexicans.

"They united in order to see their common enemy defeated. I was told that men had been alerted all over the countryside to meet secretly in the church on the Plaza until the ringing of a midnight bell would signal an attack on the Governor's Palace where Price was quartered. News leaked out just in time to save the garrison, Christmas night."

"Who wanted to warn Price if he were so disliked?" asked Samuel.

"It was rumored that a mulatto servant girl was seen entering the Palace late in the evening with a plate of holiday cake to present to the Colonel. There's a suspicion that a warning note might have been folded up in the napkin. Price barely had time to order out the artillery to quell the rumored revolt."

"Did you say that a mulatto woman went to the Palace? There is just one such person in Santa Fe, I know that for a fact. She serves Dona Tules in the kitchen at the monte parlor and perhaps – perhaps performs other duties as well." Samuel didn't finish explaining in detail. The men around him snickered.

"Is Tules the woman who loaned money to Colonel Mitchell?" asked Lt. Lea. His expression showed a dawning realization of intrigue.

"Of course she is! Tules was making double sure that Armijo would never have a chance to return to Santa Fe," answered Magoffin. "Her jealous anger was Price's salvation."

A few days later on January 22, 1847, the long awaited arrival of Major Meriweather Clark with army cannon for El Paso reaffirmed that the situation was now much more desperate than any of them had feared. He stated that even though the revolt of December 25 was unsuccessful, there were still pockets of very determined unrest to the north. Susan wrote in her diary, "we might all have been killed long before this." Samuel was advised to leave immediately to join the other wagons farther south. Dr. Richardson, his wagoner and the escort of soldiers were also urged to leave with the Magoffins.

"Sir, I hate to tell you the circumstances that prompt my urging," Major Clark explained to the worried Samuel. "We received word on the night of January 19 a mob, infuriated by the sheriff's refusal to release two Pueblo Indians from the Taos jail, calmly murdered that same sheriff, the town prefect and a Mexican bystander who had yelled a warning to them. Drunk and delirious with vengeance, they proceeded to Governor Bent's house in Taos where more angry men joined them in battering at the wall and heavy door. The governor stood within, pleading for understanding and a chance to negotiate. He had always been friendly to the Pueblos and hoped he could reason with them. The frenzied mob would not listen to Bent but climbed on the roof, dug a hole through it and dropped down into the patio just as Mrs. Bent and their three children with her sister, married to Kit Carson, were being pulled through the common adobe wall which separated them from the adjoining house. The women had literally dug their way with iron kitchen spoons and a fireplace poker through the thick mud wall."

"Didn't Bent try to follow them?"

"He didn't have time, for the Indians swarmed over him, scalping him alive, then shooting and stabbing him innumerable times. It was a horrid crime. The governor was unarmed."

The men stood silent as Major Clark concluded his hair-raising tale. Each wondered if perhaps they had waited too long to flee, if perhaps a similar bloody fate might befall their small party before they could reach the main army train.

Samuel, white-lipped and tense, said to Susan: "Let's pack up and leave immediately, today."

"We'll divide up our money and each of us will wear it around our waists," Samuel told his brother William who was helping them prepare the wagons. Samuel added, "Susan will hang the cloth sack of small coins under her skirt and the soldiers will wear a share of Magoffin money belts too. At least until we reach camp tomorrow night."

There was no sleep or rest for any of them. William and Samuel staggered from the weight of boxes and guns and ammunition. The soldiers and teamsters had their own weapons, but the Magoffins' unused guns had to be cleaned, loaded and packed securely in the carriage basket for their use. Susan handled them gingerly at first, but soon grew accustomed to the chore under the dire necessity for haste. Before daylight they had prepared a double-barreled shotgun, a pair of holster guns, several pistols and a Colt six-barrel revolver for her own use.

After a bone-wearying journey she noted in her journal the next night that they were at last mentally and physically prepared to defend themselves. Living with constant uncertainty had made her resigned to whatever fate should befall them. She calculated that they had traveled only eight miles through deep sand, but by February 1, they were at last safe in their tent again. "How exceedingly cold it is," she wrote, "water froze to a thickness of an inch and a half in a cup on our table last night. The inmates of the bed suffered though under a buffalo robe, a counterpane and three pairs of Mackenaw blankets.

By the goodness of God we have come this far in safety. One month of this year is gone and eight months since we started on this long journey. I wonder if I shall ever get home again. But 'tis all the same if I do or do not.''

9

The arid area known as *Jornada del Muerto* in southern New Mexico is, any season of the year, a dry expanse of stunted growth, bordered by the Fray Cristobal Range. Here the Rio Grande begins to flow wide in a westward curve, flanked by rugged hills. Traveling through deep, shifting sand was a formidable task for the heavily loaded wagons. Samuel had to halt his caravan, double the ox teams hitched to each wagon, and goad the over-taxed animals over the almost impassable terrain. Susan shuddered, as she always did, when "whipping out" was the only way to force the animals to pull. They could scarcely cover a few yards until even the hardest-hearted teamsters call a halt to rest.

Susan rode listless in the battered Rockaway carriage, its shiny black paint dulled by wind-driven sand, its wheels patched and mended and its broken top reinforced with assorted short studs of used lumber. Her mood matched the surroundings, or perhaps the bleak landscape itself created her feeling of despair and sadness.

Depression shadowed her shoulders; she seriously wondered if she would ever see her home again. She spent more time with her Bible, not only seeking guidance for herself but new assurances with which she could comfort her husband and his weary men.

However, when she read of the wanderings of the Tribes of Israel through sandy desert wastes, she felt ashamed of her own rebellious heart. She was tired of meeting crisis after daily crisis. She was tired of knowing that tomorrow things would probably be worse. She also wondered about the strange force within masculine hearts which drove them to leave security in search of riches or power.

At the regular camping ground at Fray Cristobal not even a lone adobe broke the barren stretches. A little grass, a little water in the river gave the last vestiges of sustenance to their half-starved livestock. For humans who had dreaded the nearly 80 miles of desert, the Jornada was now a fearful reality. It was at this point that the trail was blocked from the river course by rocky hills. It straggled south again to meet the river, but there was no surface water between the two points. Sometimes in winter a light snow or drizzling rain might provide temporary relief for the thirsty trail animals.

At the first camp a high wind almost demolished their tattered tent, sifting sand over their cooking pots and food. Susan wound her veil tightly over her face and neck. It was a struggle to hold down the tin eating utensils against the howling fury of the icy blasts. The patient animals bowed their heads and turned tails into the gale. They made little attempt to graze but stood unmoving and miserable.

Francisco was the only one who didn't grit his teeth. He and Ring frisked from wagon to wagon with careless concern. Comapu huddled over the flickering fire that first blazed with a flash of sparks, then almost died as the wind scattered his hoard of small sticks and grass. "Stay close to the wagons, *muchacho*," he called, but the words were blown away across the sand. Francisco romped gaily toward the hills.

"Fuego, fuego, fire, fire!" A childish scream of warning rose thinly above the wind. "*Fuego, abajo de carro!*" Near the baggage wagon a wind-blow flame spread its thin red line toward the wheels. It sputtered out when the boy stamped vigorously, his brown legs flying in a mighty effort.

"*Bueno, bueno,*" the men applauded and turned back to their work.

In a few minutes another frantic shout split the air, this time from Gabriel. "*Ayuda*, help, *aqui!*"

Francisco had put out the first fire, but he had also kicked away a charred bit of weed which flamed anew with the next gust. This time glowing sparks had landed in a circle of sparse grass and dry chaparral. It burst upward with a roar, sending hot ash and bits of burning stems over the entire camp. A dozen fires leaped and spread within the circled wagons. Wind-driven smoke blinded choking teamsters who pushed and strained in a massive effort to save their goods.

"Over here, over here," shouted Samuel. "This wagon holds our gunpowder. Push it clear. Push, push, push."

A fire on the prairie is chiefly limited to burning grass. But the ammunition wagon was another matter. At Samuel's warning, the teamsters deserted their wagons, and all hands, by desperate effort, rolled the ammo wagon clear.

"Francisco, where are you?" Susan peered through the smoke. "Ring, here boy!" She tried to find them. When they didn't answer she knew that the dog would protect the child and pull him out of danger of the licking flames. Choking and blinded by smoke she saw blankets, sticks, ox-whips flash in the air as men beat at the ever-spreading fire.

Every blade of grass was precious. The cattle would die if they couldn't graze before setting out on the Jornada. With that superhuman effort that lies under the skin of all men in time of crisis, the wagoners somehow brought the fire under control. Samuel posted guards for the rest of the night. Their supper which had been started earlier had burned itself to black crusts. They went to bed hungry, grimy, exhausted.

During the night when the wind ceased its restless moaning, a clear February moon rose over the desert as if to assure the camp that there was always a tomorrow, holding promise for a better day than the one just ended. Sometimes, however, it seemed an empty promise.

Next morning, Susan was able to write in her journal that they were traveling a better road toward Dead Man's Lake, an alkaline depression with no water.

Friday February 5th
Travelers generally stop here and send off their animals to water at
this small spring quite a long distance too, but it is necessary as we
shall not find water again until we strike the river 40 miles ahead.

She dozed in the security of this arid stretch that even robbers and Indians dreaded to cross. It was good to hear the monotonous clop-clop of hooves and Comapu's shrill singing. Travel undertaken by the light of the moon caused her fearful apprehension. At such times too, Comapu always nodded, his head limply swaying with the rhythm of the carriage, the reins loose in this lap. He either sings by day or sleeps by night, causing me vexation at all times she thought. But at least he's still here with us, and he's singing tonight.

By the light of the same moon, other travelers were hastily marching to meet the Magoffin caravan. Samuel had sent a rider to the Pass to ask James White to meet him. He needed a trusted messenger with guard to precede them into Mexico to make discreet inquiries for news of his brother Jim who, by now, could have been executed. Samuel had to act undercover; he instructed White to assume the role of a corn buyer for the livestock. White was to proceed to the sleepy village of Dona Ana, the last settlement between the Jornada and El Paso.

By evening of the next day the caravan neared the river again, the horrors of fire and desert put aside. The fatigued oxen and mules pulled eagerly at the curly leaf grama grass, frost-bleached in winter but still nourishing at the green root clumps. It was a time of brief relaxation which Susan enjoyed. She wandered toward the rocky hillsides. Her walk over historic Indian camps renewed her sense of the age-old country they were traveling. Looking at the strange formations of the Organ Peak kindled anew her sense of adventure.

"Don't get out of sight," Samuel called toward her vanishing figure. "Stay close to the river."

She turned back to wave gaily and gestured to Francisco and Ring at his heels. "We'll be careful," she called. She knew all too well from repeated warnings that this was Apache country, but something within her wanted out of camp. To find solace in the mountain heights and vast, silent land would certainly strengthen courage for what lay ahead. She always felt an instinctive, animal-stiffening of her spine in times of great danger. She knew she must prepare for crossing the Pass and entering enemy territory. What a different person she had become from the girlish bride who started the journey. Could it possibly be just last summer? Less than a year ago?

Men in the camp also were showing the results of long strain and hardship. Susan had learned to shut her ears to their cursing, to close her eyes to dirty clothes and overgrown beards, to ignore uncouth behavior. She even privately felt inclined to excuse them for letting off steam by occasional drunkenness and brawling. However, she wasn't prepared for what happened next morning.

The whole camp was awakened before dawn by the riotous arrival of three wagoners, shouting their way back from a night's spree in Dona Ana. "Roll 'er in, boys, roll 'er in!" A shout, some damns and hells and dull metallic clanking of chains against wheels brought Samuel bounding from his tent. He walked in his long nightshirt through the dim light. "What's the matter, fellows, what's going on?"

A swaying figure on a steady horse rode up before the tent door. Bowing to the saddle before Samuel, the man called out. "I'll shay, Magof-fin, old boy, we brung you a pur-ty lil' pre-sunt."

Samuel, no stranger to liquor himself, could smell the man's breath in the cold dawn air. "A what?" he asked curiously.

"A pre-sunt, ol' iron Betsy her-shelf. Roll 'er up, boys, show 'er to our boss man."

The astounded Magoffin watched the fellow fall off his horse, stagger to join two teamsters who were puffing over a Mexican cannon. Its brass throat gleamed dully in the pale light, its heavy wheel began to sink into the sand. "God in heaven, where did you get that?"

"Me and my buddies rolled it off the plaza thas whar, off the pla-za.."

94

One of the men began to cackle. His high laugh sounded thin and reedy. "Cannon too good fer them Mex. We'll use it against them ourselves, that's for shur-tain. We'll use their own cannon against them. Whoop-ee, whoopee!"

Suddenly a crowd in various stages of undress surrounded the brass artillery piece now parked by Magoffin's tent. Will's face poked out from a wagon canvas. He grinned broadly at the sight of the three men holding themselves upright and leaning on a brass cannon barrel. "How do you suppose they got it back here?" he asked Gabriel who shook his head in disbelief.

"Hey, you two in the wagon," Samuel called, "get down and harness a team to drag this thing back to the plaza at once." The indignation in his voice slightly sobered the offenders. "You three get back to your wagons and sleep it off. Captain Hall will deal with you later."

The whole camp, awakened by the fracas, stood around while the cannon was hitched up and started back to Dona Ana. Peals of hilarious laughter echoed over the desert. Even the mules brayed loud and long to add to the pre-dawn uproar.

"Will, you and Gabriel find the *Alcalde* and apologize for me. We'll move camp down river today, keep those rascals out of further trouble. Tell him I'm sorry this happened." Samuel turned back to the tent, muttering under his breath. "Damn their hides, if it weren't so serious a matter, it might have been funny."

Susan laughed softly. "I think it's just terrible, but the men have so little diversion. I've felt myself that I might never laugh again, that is, until we get home."

That same evening James White, the corn buyer, returned with a message from Colonel Doniphan. It was the first encouraging word they'd had in weeks. "The Colonel said to tell you, sir, that he is now about 20 miles below El Paso and that his troops have cleared the Pass. To assure him safe passage and guarantee security for the traders, however, he has taken several prominent Mexican citizens hostage."

"Are you sure that the taking of hostages will not react unfavorably upon us since we are following him?" asked Samuel.

"He thinks it a proper step, sir. He has warned the people that if any U.S. citizen is harmed, the hostages will be promptly executed. His army is being very careful not to disturb the countryside."

"That's the best news I could possibly hear, unless it was that Jim had been released. Did you find any clue as to his whereabouts?"

"None at all. A few had heard he was in prison, but they didn't know where or—" Here his voice dropped to a whisper, "whether he were still alive or not."

95

True to his promise to move the train from Dona Ana, the next day Samuel advanced down river toward Brazito where the successful battle on Christmas day had occurred. While the tent was being set up and the night fire kindled, Susan rode horseback over the flat land that lay along the elbow bend of the Rio Grnde. She dismounted now and then to pick up trophies of the battle, some empty cartridges, an insignia from a Mexican uniform. She intended to add these souvenirs to her collection. I'm glad that most of my other treasures are nature's own, not man-made symbols of war, she thought.

A late express message from Colonel Price in Santa Fe arrived on its way south to Doniphan marked *Orders For The Pass Only*. Since he had already cleared the Pass, Dr. Richardson, being the only army personnel in camp, took the liberty to open the dispatch case in search of further information that might help the train in clearing entrance into Mexico. There were also newspapers from the United States that were at least two months old, but were eagerly seized upon for news of home.

Included were two letters from Susan's family telling of marriages, one death and the usual activities. "They are sorry that I ever left home at all," she told Samuel. This family attitude was not new to him, for he remembered how Mr. Shelby had violently opposed their marriage. "I didn't know we would have so much trouble or be delayed so many times myself," he confessed. "I'll count it God's blessing if we get back safely by the end of this year."

Susan now had another personal worry, as great as her fear for their safety. This time she was quick to suspect the same symptoms she had first experienced last July. She had noticed when she dismounted from her horse that her head swam and her breath was short. She had to lean against her mount to regain composure. During the next few days she remained in the tent. Samuel noticed this and commented.

"Are you finally acting with discretion and not wandering away from camp as you usually do?"

"Oh, it's Sunday, and I thought it would be better to read my Bible than ride aimlessly around."

Samuel noticed that she seemed quite subdued, perhaps a little pale. "We've had good news, Susanita, with Doniphan's unchallenged advance. Cheer up, we'll cross the Rio Grande tomorrow and catch up with him in no time. The travel will be much easier from now on."

True to his prediction they did have a quick, uneventful crossing, fording at a shallow place where the wagons weren't endangered as they had often been by the high steep banks of mountain rivers. Thus far they hadn't been attacked by either Mexicans or Indians, had not used their guns in self protection, and had crossed the Jornada without serious incident. For these things they were profoundly grateful, although they had mentally prepared themselves to meet any or all of them. The long drawn out suspense had been very unnerving to the whole camp.

Shortly after they reached the Mexican side of the river, they received word that they were awaited at the home of Don Agapita and his daughter Josefita. This cultured gentleman, a son of Old Spain, was a long-time friend of the Magoffin brothers. He expressed much concern and sympathy for Samuel when told of James' capture and imprisonment. His daughter, likewise gracious in typical Old World fashion, was charmed with the little wife, *pequena esposa*. Susan felt satisfaction with the cordiality that had been extended her husband in towns and villages all along the way.

To the trail-worn Magoffins, Don Agapita's spacious house and garden seemed blessed with heavenly beauty and peace. The white-washed walls were decorated with hand painted flowers. Realistic vines on trellises smothered the door frames with all season greenness. This tropical decoration was quite different from the calico-covered walls in casas in Santa Fe. Bird cages hung from small trees planted among flower beds in the patio. Pigeons fluttered to the stone floor to pick up grains of corn scattered around the grinding stone. Susan glimpsed garden and fruit trees with grape arbors already budding in the warmth of late February days.

They ate on a schedule that scarcely left time between each repast for appetites to be whetted. Susan managed to taste some of each of the well-prepared boiled meat dishes as well as the usual vegetable accompaniments of tomatoes, cabbage and onions. Samuel noticed how she picked at her food, but he ate generous portions of all that was served. After trail fare, each meal was a delight to him.

Don Agapita was much intrigued with their stories. "Tell me, Senora Susana, just how it is that you have made such an arduous journey and still have survived? It is most unusual for a young lady of your social standing to travel thus."

"My husband has taken good care of me, assisted at times by the Good Lord above." She smiled at his question, the same one many others had asked before.

"There is no book or teacher who could have enlightened you about this part of the world like seeing it firsthand. Experiences teaches in the best way, though not always the easiest." he observed.

"I left home to travel; to make a different life from that in Kentucky, True, it has been very hard at times, but I have no regrets."

It was a paradox that they were so well received by natives within enemy territory. Samuel kept reminding her, "These people have been my friends for many years, and since the war is little understood by Mexican citizens, they feel no disloyalty by maintaining friendly relations with us."

Susan would have preferred to remain in the casa of Don Agapita for she enjoyed conversation with the kindly, philosophical old gentleman. However, plans had been made for a more permanent accommodation in the home of Reverendo Ramon Ortiz, the curate of El Paso del Norte. A fiery patriot who had been stirring up opposition among the villagers, he was one of the hostages taken by Colonel Doniphan to strengthen the position of the army. Another paradox, it seemed to Susan, was that their presence in the home of a hostage would be accepted by the citizens. What a crazy, mixed-up war!

She had the companionship of Ortiz' two sisters, his niece and three children. She was drawn to the beautiful, well-mannered little girls as she was to all children, and they in turn to her. They sat at her feet in the sunny patio, begging for *mas historias*, more stories.

Susan found herself the object of polite solicitations from the servants, starting with the serving of morning chocolate in her room, continuing throughout the day until the evening meal at nine o'clock. With many to share the work, the bustle of this household intrigued her. She declared that she would like to collect some of their fine recipes and was overwhelmed with directions for preparing every kind of dish. She also had many personal callers, some frankly curious about the Americana, but all much more polite and mannerly than the villagers of northern New Mexico. She in turn told them about food preparation and housekeeping in the States. She welcomed the change of scene and conversation. How good to be a woman among women again!

She dressed in one of her New York gowns to accompany her hostesses to Mass, feeling that the act of worship itself was important, that the place, whether Catholic cathedral or Protestant church or even her own room, was only secondary to expressing faith. "Won't you go with us today, Samuel? We are guests in the home of the curate, and I think you ought to."

"You go, Susanita; pray for both of us. I feel that if I keep my trade wagons open in the plaza today I may pick up information about Jim. People who come by to look at my wares stay to chat and pass the time of day. The Lord will forgive me, I hope. You ask Him to."

Susan gave him a reproachful look and joined the senoras for the short walk to the little adobe church. Everywhere the air was perfumed with orange and fruit blossoms. Susan glanced about her with appreciation for the beauty of the village church and this Sabbath morning, so different from the one she had spent last week on the Jornada. Her life, it seemed, alternated between extreme danger and peaceful delights.

Monday brought many visitors curious to examine the elaborate brocade material of her Sunday dress and the details of its trim and cut. Susan held a miniature fashion show in her room, unpacking a number of her dresses, bonnets and shawls. "May I borrow this one?" asked Dona Francisca, a talented lady noted for her fine embroidery.

"We don't plan to be here more than a few days. You're welcome to the dress until that time."

"*Si, poco tiempo*, just a little while, Senora Magoffin. I wish to cut off the pattern to make a dress for my daughter. She is about your size and age. How old are you?"

"Nineteen," answered Susan, "almost twenty."

The senoras all exchanged looks of admiration for the young American who had come into their midst, speaking their own language and adopting their food and customs.

However, for Susan the days of peace and pleasure began to be marred by headaches, nausea and the unmistakable signs of pregnancy. She was glad that she was still able to conceive a child after the disastrous accident of last summer. Ripples of dismay spread into unwelcome realization. How untimely! How worried Samuel will be, she said to herself, and this time I'll have to tell him right away. There's not a chance for me to pick a romantic place or special time like I did last summer. Now I'll just try to find an opportunity when he's not so filled with anxiety about his wagons, about Jim, even about me.

Because her journal was getting short of paper, Susan began to make only terse entries concerning the next weeks' events. Undoubtedly she was also growing afraid that her written comments, as Samuel had repeatedly warned, would be crucially incriminating if they were taken prisoners. She feared that the very ladies who had come to call might be the first to search her possessions as a spy.

By March 1, news spread over the entire village that General Wool was blockaded at Monterrey, that troops were marching up from Durango to join the Chihuahua attack on Colonel Doniphan, that Santa Ana was preparing to invade Texas and that the American forces were greatly outnumbered, their artillery insufficient.

How many times they had heard such rumors. Yet, not to take them seriously would be foolhardy and dangerous. No one could say where the latest fighting was taking place or whether the battle had been won or lost. News was tardy, inaccurate, always alarming.

Although Samuel daily sold much merchandise, he began to feel that his attempts to ferret out news of Jim under cover of his trade was extremely risky. He didn't confess to Susan that he had been privately warned of a plot to confiscate their wagons and imprison them both. Casually on the third of March he said, "I think I'll bring the wagons into the plaza today and place them under the protection of the civil authority that Doniphan set up when he left."

Susan replied, "I'll stay in our room, I think. Even though the family of Reverendo Ortiz remains cordial, I'm beginning to be afraid for their sakes as well as my own. I can sense the change in temper of our visitors. They seem to be spying on me instead of coming to chat in the friendly way they did when we first arrived. They're listening for me to drop news of our army."

"You're right, Susanita. Stay in your room; I won't be gone long. I'll leave the actual moving of wagons to Will and Captain Hall. It's best that I remain here with you. A mob is terrifying when aroused."

"A mob?" Susan clung to him. "To think that we've come to this. I wish I were safely back with my mother and our old family doctor. I've been dreading to tell you, mi alma, I know how worried, how much care – but I must tell you now. Our second child is on the way. It will be born on foreign soil instead of in Kentucky." She laid her head on his shoulder and wept.

His grasp tightened around her as the realization of her unexpected news shook his stalwart frame. "Susanita, not now, to think I have caused you this extra burden. Oh my dearest, my dearest..."

"What can we do? Where can we turn?" She brushed hot tears with the back of her hand.

Samuel gently guided her to the bed. "Rest now, dearest, I'll be back as quickly as I can."

10

Susan stared at the painted flowers on her bedroom wall. The decorations that had seemed so gay and appealing when she first arrived now looked garish. She was numb, past weeping, almost past caring.

True to his promise her husband returned before noon. No matter their fate, they agreed it must be shared. As they sat, hand in hand, looking at the blossoming trees, Susan said, "Such peace in the garden; such tumult in our hearts."

They were startled by a shadowy figure who had slipped unnoticed to the entrance of their bedroom. A perspiring, breathless man leaned against the doorframe. "Senor," he cried urgently, "Senor, I must see you alone." He jerked his head in Susan's direction. They recognized him as Don Rouquia, a friend of the curate.

"Step in here," Samuel gestured toward a small storeroom. Don Rouquia hestiated. "Can anyone else hear? I would be hanged as a traitor if I were caught bringing military news to an Americano!"

"There is no one. We are alone," Magoffin assured him.

"Mi amigo, I am a loyal Mexicano. It pains me to tell you –" Susan strained her ears to hear his low whisper.

"It gives me *mucho dolor*, much sorrow –" his voice broke.

For Susan the suspense became unbearable. She noticed her husband wiping his perspiring brow. He blinked his eyes rapidly.

"The Americanos have routed my countrymen! In a severe battle, on February 28, on the Sacramento River. Doniphan took Chihuahua."

"What of my brother? Have you news of him?"

Rouquia shook his head. "No news of Don Santiago, but el Senor Ortiz is safe. I go to tell his sisters. Are they here?'

Samuel could hear Susan catch her breath in a tremulous sigh. "In the kitchen," she directed the messenger.

There was no more need for secrecy. Don Rouquia darted back into the curtained hallway, made his way to the front door where he paused to call loudly, "Dona Ana, Dona Rosalita, where are you?"

Susan could hear his shouts of gladness. "Your brother, el Senor Cura, is safe! He's at the trader camp outside Chihuahua."

Both women then rushed into the hall, shrieking their joy. A jumble of words, tearful exclamations, questions filled the room. Running feet of the children made rhythmical echoes down the hall.

"Praise be to the Holy Father!" Then a sudden silence, a rustling of skirts. The relieved women sank to their knees in prayers of thanks.

Susan looked up at her husband. "I'm so happy for them, so happy. It renews my hope for our brother."

"Indeed it does," Samuel leaned over to give her a quick hug. "It will be hard to wait for the official news, but I'll wager that Doniphan's ragged Missourians fought with valor."

The village of El Paso rocked with rumors like the aftershock of an earthquake as couriers from the south began to arrive daily. It was reported that the curate was not at the camp but dead. A letter from Don Sebastian to his wife told of complete American victory with only James Owens, a major in the organized traders' army, killed. One trader died from his wounds and seven others were slightly hurt. The Mexicans were routed with casualties of 300 and about the same number wounded.

American forces gave the 40 prisoners humane and decent treatment. Another courier on March 9 declared that the curate was on the way home, that James Magoffin was *alive* and had been moved to a prison in Durango as the Mexican army retreated farther south. Susan wept with joy over Jim, with sorrow over their friend James Owens. He was a man of much influence and sound judgment, who had been a great help to the Magoffin brothers over a period of several years.

During succeeding days, Samuel was kept informed of the situation. He learned that a large amount of spoils, food, wine, ammunition, cannon, blankets and a military chest filled with copper coins were recovered from the battle field. Samuel was told an incredible story about finding a thousand ropes, each already tied with a noose, with which the Mexicans had intended to lead American prisoners back to Mexico City. In addition, the Missourians captured the same black flag with its skull and cross bones that had floated over the enemy troops at Brazito. He did not tell Susan the gory details of the rout, the way Americans sabered Mexicans on the run, chasing them into the river, running some the whole 15-mile distance back to Chihuahua, shooting those who fell. War certainly dehumanizes the best of men, he thought.

On March 10, the family of the curate had a direct answer to their prayers. Their brother appeared at his own doorway, unharmed and smiling. The Magoffins joined in their homecoming festivities and heard him recount other details of the battle.

With such positive assurances that the way to Chihuahua was now clear, Samuel gave word to his company of wagons to be ready to leave El Paso the following day. It was Sunday, but this time Susan made no complaint about the lack of church attendance. She was as eager as her husband to be gone.

During their stay in El Paso, Susan had temporarily forgotten how the jolting of the carriage had shaken her bones. Now she was vividly reminded of every rock and rut each time they bumped over acequias, the network of ditches that crisscrossed the river trail. She looked forward to the quiet of the night to be spent in whatever accommodations Samuel could arrange. The places might be crude, but it was less risky than camping in the open tent.

Time and again she had to refuse the highly seasoned food thrust upon her by well-meaning senoras who rented them a room. "*Gracias, no mas*, thank you, no more, *gracias*," she repeated to each hostess.

For three torrid weeks they traveled through rocky, sandy terrain that required numerous rest stops for the broken down ox and mule teams. The fine dust was suffocating. Her veil was too stiff with dust accumulated from Missouri to Mexico for her to wear any longer. Their hours of sleep were erratic and limited.

Susan lost track of the days. "Is this Monday or Tuesday?" she asked her husband. "We were up before dawn, traveling a bit, sleeping a bit, stopping so many times, and now it is dark again. I scarcely know whether it is today's dawn or yesterday's dusk. Tell me, what is it?"

Excessive heat sapped their energy. Their clothes grew stiff with sweat. Susan wrote in her diary:

> *Thursday, April 1*
> *Our travels are now made altogether after night on account of the heat. Though it is not very agreeable to me, as my head and stomach are somewhat delicate of late, I came to travel and therefore take it patiently, as a custom of the road.*

A more sinister kind of heat, that of back fires set to burn off tall grass, was now a customary precaution in each camp after the near disaster of the prairie fire some weeks ago. The only breaks in the daily monotony were the constant complaints of a Dutchman who was with them. His voluble, broken English amused them all. A Frenchman, incongruously named "Don Santiago," fumed over a bad trade when he felt cheated for his pair of "hoxen." Moreover, the bawdy jokes of Irish Pat easily shocked the still prudish Susan. Men, in their extremities, have a way of laughing off danger and inconvenience wherever they find themselves, Susan thought, and forgave Pat his improper talk.

Spring had come to the desert, though with little rain, and the terrain looked just as barren as in any other season. Susan didn't want rain or flowers or trees or anything, just rest. She thought about her stubborn eagerness when she embarked on the journey, how the excitement had changed to danger, how only constant discomfort remained. She felt she was not the same carefree person who had set out so gaily last summer. Now all she wanted was to go home, but she gritted her teeth in new determination to persevere to the end, whenever it might come.

On the 4th of April, the Magoffin wagons, following about two weeks behind the army, creaked their way into Chihuahua, the merchant's paradise, their original goal, after ten months on the way. Doniphan had not enjoyed his role of father protector to the rowdy bunch of teamsters who had traveled with him. And the Magoffins were definitely not prepared for what they found upon reaching the ancient city after the traders.

While the commander had been occupied with tedious trade arrangements as well as necessary councils of war, his Volunteers, lacking the discipline of regular troops, had taken over the town. Ignoring the assurance that General Kearny had given at Santa Fe, that the army was a protector not a conqueror, the First Missourians seized private dwellings, bathed in the public fountain, chopped down trees along the public *alameda* and swaggered through the parks with a senorita on each arm. Their wages were still unpaid. Therefore they took what they wanted. Their drunkenness kept the citizens in a state of alarm day and night. News of General Wool's victory at Buena Vista on February 22 gave new impetus to their uninhibited celebratory behavior.

"I don't like the looks of this," Samuel remarked as they drove through the demolished plaza.

Susan recalled the neat uniforms, the clean appearance of General Kearny's army. "Those fellows lounging against the wall look like ruffians, not soldiers, even if they did come from good old Missouri."

They halted near a public building familiar to Samuel. He entered and within a short time, using his prestige as a well-known merchant, had secured a decent dwelling for Susan and himself.

The Rockaway stopped in front of an adobe house a block from the plaza. Samuel dismounted and lifted Susan down, "Yet another house, dearest, but this one we'll have all to ourselves."

Susan's weary face brightened with her quick smile. "That's all I could ask for – a bed, any kind of bed."

To Susan's grateful surprise, it was the largest, most beautiful house they had yet stayed in. The morning after they arrived she walked from room to room, admiring the elaborate wall decorations, the iron grillwork at the deeply recessed windows, the woven floor coverings. Each room opened upon the central patio now in the fullness of tropic bloom. There were shade trees, some showing flowers she had never seen before. A small pool bore water lilies lifting gold and pink cups to the pure blueness of the sky.

"I'll leave Comapu and Francisco here with you," Samuel explained after a hurried breakfast, "while I contact Hall to see where he has located the wagons. I need to give instructions about opening up today for trade." Opening for trade! How long he had awaited this time. He smiled gaily, like his old self.

She responded to his enthusiasm with a great goodbye hug and kiss. If a man's excited about his business, she thought, he believes the world will take care of itself.

She called Comapu who had been unpacking a hamper of summer clothes. Could it be a whole year had passed since she had first selected these garments for their use here in Chihuahua? She counted out coins into his outstretched palm, "You and Francisco each take a basket to the market. Select fruit, any kind that looks good – mangoes, oranges, lemons, papayas. Also look for a new shirt and sandals for Francisco."

The boys grinned at her, their dark eyes alight, for they had been eager to see the town ever since yesterday. The two set off at a gallop. She knew that Comapu wanted to stay in Mexico when they returned to the States, and now that Francisco had become so firmly attached to the older boy, she hoped that Samuel would make financial arrangements for his care in order for them to remain together.

She busied herself in the kitchen, checking the few utensils the owners had left. She decided to ask Samuel that night to find a *comadre* to help with housework as she was sure they would be in Chihuahua some time, at least until most of the merchandise could be sold. That is, if no enemy attack prevented.

As soon as work circulated about the American woman who had arrived with the last group of wagons, visitors began to call, just as they had done in the other places where they stayed. This time Susan welcomed them, especially Don Pedro Olivares who had visited the United States. He spoke English with the same limitations that Susan spoke Spanish. He was a jolly man who laughed a great deal and openly admired the *Americana* who had defied custom to become a traderess.

"Would you like to remain in Mexico? Your husband could trade from here in Chihuahua to Santa Fe," the Don said in hesitant, awkwardly phrased English.

"*Senor, que imposible!*" she answered in his native language.

"Our country is beautiful and living is easy, if you have the means to live well, and your husband evidently has much wealth."

"*Me da la mismo*, it is all the same to me, in America, in Chihuahua. *Me quedo con el*, I stay with him."

"You are a good wife," replied the Don, "a good little wife."

Indeed Susan had been a good wife through all the months of hardship and danger. She smiled at his compliment, then fell silent wondering if Samuel had really considered staying indefinitely in Chihuahua. Though it was a hot, sultry day, she shivered at the prospect, knowing that his diligence with his trade might indeed include such a plan.

It was with the family of John Potts, the English consul and President of the Silver Mint, that Susan found real companionship. Their summer home in late April was a bower of jacaranda and poinsianna trees. A high hedge of flaming hibiscus surrounded the garden. When Susan arrived there to visit them, she was struck with the tropical beauty of the adobe hacienda, its cool front portal lined with fragrant pots of geranium and gardenias. Tooled leather chairs stood against the wall, inviting rest from the sunshine. A garden of Eden, she thought gratefully.

Her eyes adjusted to the dim coolness of the *sala* where the elaborately dressed hostesses rustled taffeta petticoats when they rose to greet her. Though the room was furnished in traditional Spanish style, a gleaming golden harp beside a handsome square piano caught her eye immediately. After greetings and polite conversation, Susan impulsively walked to the keyboard to strike a few soft chords. With shining eyes she turned to her hostess, "It's been so very, very long since I've heard any music except camp songs and a guitar. Won't you please play?"

The consul's wife and her sister were just as happy to entertain Susan as she was to enjoy their feminine company. They played the old ballads and love songs, inviting her to join them. Too soon it was time for *la merienda*, the traditional serving of chocolate and sweet cakes in late afternoon.

Consul Potts arrived home during Susan's visit. Like his wife he was intrigued with their young visitor who related some of her trail adventures to their astonishment and wonder. "We lead such secluded lives, we're a trifle envious of your adventures," Mrs. Potts remarked.

"Now it's your turn to tell me of what has happened in Chihuahua since Doniphan advanced into the city," Susan replied.

"You can see the disastrous results of the occupation in our plaza," Potts answered, a frown drew his thick blonde eyebrows together and his mouth into a straight line.

"Yes, I know, it's shameful, positively shameful, the way our troops behaved. They are an undisciplined lot of soldiers."

"I had an experience myself with Colonel Mitchell, who was acting under orders of war to search all the wealthy homes for contraband and concealed arms. He sent a messenger to my place for the key to the residence of Governor Trias who had escaped with his family when the army took over."

Susan nodded, recalling the daring of this same Colonel Mitchell in escorting Dona Tules to the officer's ball in Santa Fe. She remembered the rumor that her cash had outfitted the army.

"I refused to surrender the key," stated the Consul very positively. "I had been left in charge of the official residence, and since I represented the British government, not the American, I disregarded his request."

"Did he accept your decision – without vociferous objection, that is," asked Susan, remembering Mitchell's brusque manner.

"He certainly did not. Within a short time the man brought back a terse reply that the Colonel had a *key* which would open all doors and that he would carry out his order with his howitzers – his military key."

"What a useless destruction that would have been," exclaimed Susan. "I've seen the Governor's Residence, and it is truly a beautiful and stately establishment."

"My brother was occupying the home during the Governor's absence, and I feared for his life if Colonel Mitchell gave the command to fire that cannon. I would be responsible to the Mexican government for allowing such wanton destruction," explained Mr. Potts.

"Did you hand over the key?"

"With much reluctance, my dear, with much reluctance, but the army search found nothing in the house but personal possessions of the official family. They withdrew with no damage being done."

"Colonel Mitchell is a daring, almost ruthless officer," replied Susan. "Now I'll tell you what I know about him." She regaled the family with an animated account of the Santa Fe ball and of the shock Dona Tules' appearance had on the proper senoras.

"War creates much confusion amid the customs of ordinary living," stated the Consul. "We are in no danger, but still my family has restricted their activities and visits in the town."

Susan's carriage at the door was announced. "We're so glad to make your acquaintance, Mrs. Magoffin," the consul's wife and her sister exclaimed. "Do visit us again."

She assured them of her delight at the thought of another call. She made mental note that she would wear her very best dress on the next occasion, even though its heavy grosgrain bodice required tightlacing to reduce her now slightly enlarged waistline to the proper slenderness.

That night during their simple supper which Susan had prepared herself, she told her husband of the afternoon's visit. "I'd like to see those English ladies as often as I can," she concluded. She waited a bit, then asked, "How long do you think we will stay in Chihuahua?" She held her breath, steeling herself for his answer.

"Until I sell all my merchandise, I hope," replied her husband. "I'm sure we traders will have to follow military orders, and I have no way of knowing. Of course, you realize that I won't *ever* leave Mexico until I've made every effort to secure Jim's release from prison."

"There's no assurance you can do that, is there, unless you go to Durango yourself?"

"That's too far south from our route to Saltillo. I have no choice, Susan, but to follow Doniphan's army. Whenever it marches, we march too and will depend on couriers for news. Be prepared to leave at any time. We won't have much notice, you know."

Be prepared to leave! What a familiar ring those words had to Susan. She always complied as quickly as possible, having packed and repacked countless times. On April 25 a scout returned with an order for the troops to join General Zachary Taylor. The army set out, one division at a time, toward the southern coast where some of the unpaid troops, whose volunteer enlistment was up, would embark for the United States. A few traders decided to remain in Chihuahua to finish selling their goods before returning to Santa Fe. They had had enough of war. Some of them, in too big a hurry to wait, sold goods at a discount. But Samuel wasn't one of these. Driven by his zeal to release his brother, the Magoffin wagons set out three days later.

Susan did not write in her journal from April 1 to May 23rd when she confessed that she had no words of description to tell of the forced march south.

> *Saltillo May 23*
>
> *I must first say I trust fortune will never compel me to make the same kind of trip again. I thought I had done some hard travelling before, and in truth I had, but this has surpassed all. We travelled regularly 20, to 30 or 35 miles each day for three weeks, resting but two days of the time and over the worst roads I ever saw.*

Through the mountainous terrain of the Rio Conchas, the Rio Florida, the rocky desert canyons between bare, sharp peaks,, they urged the teams in single file. It was 675 tortuous miles from Chihuahua to Buena Vista. Because of the suffocating dust stirred up by the army, Samuel drove his carriage at a stiff pace, slightly in the lead.

"The poor animals," Susan protested to Samuel at the end of a particularly exhausting day.

"The poor men who drive them," he replied.

Their camps were made on dry land and in swamps, their bedfellows often lizards and scorpions. There were no roads, only ruts through rocks and deep tracks in sand made by the heavy artillery and loaded commissary wagons of the army. There was little to look at along the way but dwarfed acacia bushes, thick-leaved Spanish bayonet and tall palmillo. This rocky land was as monotonous as the sandy prairie.

The news that General Winfield Scott had landed with troops at Vera Cruz and his later victory at Cerro Gordo brought them new encouragement, for they hoped this might be a decisive turning point for the American army. Samuel kept abreast of developments through his couriers who also sought undercover word of James. They were sure that he was still imprisoned at Durango and word filtered back that he was furnishing champagne by the case to jailers and town officials.

"That's just like Jim," Samuel told her. "If there's a way to enjoy a situation, no matter how desperate, he'll find it."

Susan couldn't be as cheerful, but then she didn't know Jim as well as her husband. She wondered how it would be to be married to him instead of steady, solemn Samuel. She knew she was very fond of him, and just as concerned. She wondered how many miles, how many more nights. Their food and water were limited now; the heat grew more oppressive. Daily reports of guerrilla reprisals stirred up by General Taylor's invasion of Coahuila alarmed even the trail-hardened men.

All during the journey Samuel had worn his holster and gun. His men were well-armed and Susan kept her pistols in the carriage basket.

However, the coincidence of events, the poignancy of human relations, the quick response of Colonel Doniphan to a Mexican national's warning, possibly saved the Magoffins from a truly disastrous encounter with Canales, the guerrilla chief. Being alerted that he was in the province, Doniphan hastily dispatched Lt. Gordon with 60 men to warn Samuel. That afternoon when he saw a cloud of dust swirling up in the distance, he reined in his horse toward the Rockaway. Were those guerrillas approaching?

"Susan, get out your pistols. Hand Comapu a gun too. Fasten the carriage curtains. Don't look out or leave the carriage, no matter what happens, understand!" He shouted directions to the Indian boy and whirled to warn the drivers behind them.

As she fished for the guns in the basket, her mind raced back to the other time of alarm when she had steeled herself for armed defense. Tense and shaking, she waited, grasping a pistol in each hand, eyes fixed on the window.

She heard tumultuous shouting of men and the neighing of excited horses. Samuel barked out staccato directions to Captain Hall. It was impossible to corral the wagons, for they were too strung out along the line of march. She knew Samuel was close beside the carriage, but she couldn't see him for the dust. She braced herself and clung to the arm rest. A man's voice bellowed out. "Where's the lady? Where's Mrs. Magoffin?"

At the same moment a dark shape loomed at the window. A dusty countenance peered through the carriage curtain. Susan, white-faced and tight-knuckled, aimed her pistol toward the man, grimly waiting his first move to enter. But she saw a broad grin spread over an American officer's face. It was Lt. Gordon. He saluted, whirled from the window before Susan could speak to him, but she then cracked the curtain enough to see his troops forming a patrol all around their wagons. Limply, she leaned back against the seat. Once more she voiced a prayer of thanks while the troops led the way toward Buena Vista where General Wool was quartered.

They reached the wide plain of the former battlefield on May 22.

Here they would soon bid farewell to the Missouri Volunteers who had guarded them through the tedious journey from Santa Fe. Here the famished troops were given full rations for the first time during their enlistment. They stuffed their mouths and pockets along with their coffee pots. They drew all items except bars of soap.

One of the traders repeated to the Magoffins a story he had heard around the army supply wagon. "The only thing they refused was soap. Yessir, cleaned out all supplies but soap. Said that they'd been dirty too long to bother with washing their selves now."

"What about their filthy clothes?" asked Susan. "Wouldn't you think they'd feel better just to wear clean underclothes for a change?"

Samuel threw back his head with the first real laugh Susan had heard in weeks. "If they tried to wash those rags there'd be nothing left of them but holes to dry! Doniphan will do well to get them in line for review by General Wool this afternoon."

"You mean those exhausted men have to march in formal review, half of them in tatters, half without shoes? What is the General thinking of? Does the army expect to exact the last breath of discipline from its men, regardless of circumstances?" Susan sniffed indignantly.

"It seems General Wool does. He hasn't marched those 1,300 miles himself. His boot have no holes. His underclothes are clean enough, I'd wager, to suit you. Let's drive over to watch the show."

Across the dusty camp ground the lines were beginning to form, a straggly length of troops, seasoned by hardship, bronzed by the tropic sun, still full of fight and raring to finish this last duty, irksome as it seemed. No two men wore uniforms alike, no two had a complete outfit. Tattered jackets, pants looking strangely like Mexican outfits filched from victims, shirts without sleeves, shirts without buttons, no shirts at all. More men sported woven straw hats than belts or shoes. Only a few wore military caps. Not all even carried arms. They had been unpaid, undersupplied for months.

For a full hour the troops waited for General Wool, fuming, cursing under their breath, kicking at pebbles, slouching in the heat. While they waited, Captain Reid, acting upon the General's orders, moved from group to group, exhorting the men to stay and fight, to reenlist. "This war's not over. How are we going to advance to Mexico City if you men all leave? The General needs you –"

He didn't get to finish his plea.

"Needs us? Well, Captain, our farms, our families need us too," cried one lanky fellow who still looked more like a plowman than a soldier.

"There won't be enough crops grown to winter feed the stock. We'll barely make it home for late planting. We've given all we're gonna give, sir," shouted another.

"The government will have to feed us if we can't grow our own food," said a tall, gaunt-looking farmer.

The ragged men put a rude end to this dialogue by turning away to watch Doniphan riding up and down the lines. He snapped them to quick attention. They stood erect until he rode too far away for a reprimand, then they straggled from formation again. This Colonel had always treated his men with a certain indulgence on the trail, allowing informal dress and casual attitudes and speech. Now he, as well as the Missouri Volunteers, was on inspection from General Wool.

At last the General, in the glory of full dress uniform, every brass button reflecting the sun, his sword moving rhythmically against the gleaming flank of a well-curried stallion, his posture as straight and unyielding as a Spanish bayonet, rode toward the first line of men. He was accompanied by his staff, outfitted in equally handsome uniforms, mounted on sleek, spirited horses.

The Missouri Volunteers gaped in amazement at the splendid sight. Heads turned to follow the General's progress down the line; one fellow at the very end even stepping back a few paces to get a good view. "Attention, company," commanded Doniphan.

"Gotta see this, Colonel. Ain't never seen anything as fine as this since I volunteered," the audacious man shouted back.

Samuel guffawed. "This'll be a story to repeat when we all get back home! Imagine a dress review of half-naked men."

"Surely hate to see them leave," Susan replied. "They've accomplished so much with so little. They'll be heroes in every town and village in Missouri."

On the following morning the troops apeared for a final mustering out and delivery of equipment to Captain Washington at his Buena Vista headquarters. Samuel learned later that day that they were permitted to keep the captured Mexican cannon as a trophy of war. The troops took up march again toward Saltillo and Camargo where they would set sail through the Gulf of Mexico for New Orleans and embark on a steamboat up the Mississippi.

General Wool's commendation on their arduous duties, crowned by decisive and glorious victories of Brazito and Sacramento, would never erase the painful incidents which most of the men remembered. From farm volunteers, they had become seasoned troops in the Mexican war.

The Magoffins followed Colonel Doniphan as far as Saltillo, Samuel trading his way along at each stop. Upon reaching the town they rented another small house the last of May where they rested from their journeying.

About a month later, during which time Susan had been too exhausted to write, she made her first alarmed entry in her diary.

Saltillo, June 20th Friday
I've heard of wars and rumors of wars and have been almost in them,
but this is nearer than ever – I presume we'll have military assistance
by Tuesday morning. Our forces are small; the enemy reported to be
14,000. General Wool has ordered the citizens to form a company for
defense of the city. The battle might happen here!

A battle was expected and, as usual, reports of a huge force cast gloom over the army camp and little town. A hasty express dispatched to General Taylor for reinforcements and artillery gave them faint hope. Susan was confined to the security of their house. She was ready to flee on short notice. Samuel repeated to her a tale of miraculous escape when the General's interpreter was saved from a bullet by a small testament worn in his cap. The cap itself and one half of the book were creased by the shot which tore a path of death less than an inch from his head. "That truly was a miracle, wasn't it?" she exclaimed.

The physical exertion of sewing their extra money in heavy hide sacks, packing trunks and daily apprehension took its toll of Susan's spirits. She worried over William who had joined the citizens' group on the hills above the city. By accident she found out that Samuel had secretly secured a promise from Captain Donalson that in case of bombardment, Susan would be rescued and taken by the army to a place of safety. For himself, he would remain to protect his goods and his life as best he could. It was a time of fear, excruciating fear, for them both. Samuel often looked at her with such an expression of sadness that she herself shed tears for them both.

Again, nothing happened and again Susan gave thanks for the protection of Kind Providence. Again Samuel opened up his trade. During these days Susan's longing for home grew with the passing of each agonizing day.

Friday, July 2nd
Wrote a long letter to Mama this evening. I do wish I could have a
letter from home; how lonely it is, week after week – I never hear
from them, as if I never belonged to them – quite a new creature I
should feel, but as it is, I am perfectly isolated.

But her longing heart couldn't long forever.

On Sunday, July 4th, the Magoffins attended a camp celebration at Buena Vista with all the noise and clamor General Wool's army could muster. "How different this day is from our first July 4th," she said to her husband. "That one which started out pleasantly by our climb up Pawnee Rock, ended so disastrously. What if today –"

112

"Don't talk like that, Susan," her husband interrupted. "The situation is bad enough without imagining what else might happen."

While they were at a small dinner that night with the family of Dr. Hewitson of Saltillo, Samuel learned that Major Hunter, the quartermaster at Monterrey, wished to send his own wife back to the States with the Magoffins whenever they departed.

It was a ray of hope on Susan's bleak outlook for the future. If an army wife were put in their care, perhaps Samuel, with *two* women to urge him, might be persuaded to give up the search for Jim, sell his wagons and leave immediately.

Later Captain Rucker called to know Samuel's decision about disposing of the wagons. "I can't rid myself of my goods, just to return home," he said. "I have my brother's very large investment as well as my own to protect. What rate of discount does the government propose to offer me?"

"I can't promise anything definite, sir; it would be the best bargain I could strike with the officials. However, if I may advise you, sir, I would take whatever I could get, sacrifice it, and leave quickly. The war's not over yet, you know, and the army can't offer you traders continued and indefinite protection."

Susan listened intently as she sat with her letter box on her lap. She stole a furtive glance at her husband's grim countenance. She knew he was torn between returning for her sake and a compulsion to remain. Must a man *always* consider business before all else, she questioned. She flushed guiltily, for she knew he also waited on news from Jim.

"I'll have to figure my inventory and see how much I can afford to lose," Samuel replied. "Of course, I don't want to be foolhardy. You can't promise us an escort? Do you sincerely advise immediate sale?"

"With all my heart, Magoffin. I'd take what I could get and take the first boat to New Orleans." The Captain rose. He bowed to Susan. "May you have a pleasant journey, ma'am, whenever you set out."

Samuel escorted him to the door. "I'll send word very soon, Captain. Thank you for whatever help you can give me in selling out."

She didn't wait for him to speak. With flying feet and outspread arms, she raced to embrace him. "Oh, darling, we're going home at last! Thank you, thank you!" She began to smother him with kisses of joy.

"Susanita, I guess the decision, now that it has finally made or has been made for me, is a relief. But of course there's still my brother. I still have hope."

Susan's spirits in the next few days were brightened by daily drives through the town. She saw the convent where the army was quartered, the gardens, the extensive haciendas, the elaborately decorated church and through these pleasures enjoyed a more normal life. However, her respite of calm was soon shattered by dreadful news in a letter written by a Spaniard and relayed to the Magoffins' casa by an English friend. They read that Jim had been released from the Durango prison, but that he had been *murdered* in his own bed by an unknown assailant. They held the hastily scrawled message between them, their hands trembling in horror.

The paper fluttered to the floor when Samuel groaned and fell heavily against a chair. He beat the table with clenched fists, unable to control himself. "The worst has happened, the very worst!"

Susan let him weep. Her own tears fell upon his thinning hair when she bent down to console him.

11

After a time Samuel pushed unsteadily from the table. Grim lines distorted his face with fear and grief. He stacked two trunks against the door and clicked fast the shutter locks inside the protective window grill work. "We'd better stay inside," he cautioned Susan.

Through nightmarish days they existed, jumping at each knock at the door, tiptoeing and whispering during the long hours alone. They solaced each other with false hopes until a messenger from Chihuahua brought word that an eye-witness to the murder had identified Jim's mutilated body. Now their grief changed to dry-mouthed fear for their own lives.

Samuel resorted to pre-dawn trips to his shop, returning to their room before the rest of the town stirred. Susan didn't venture out at all. Once he brought back a packet of old letters from Kentucky which they reread until each page was memorized. Even these didn't lift Susan's mood of despondency. "My family's world is monotonous with carefree living; ours with danger and suspense," she said.

Her grief brought an adverse reaction to her advancing pregnancy.

In her journal she wrote:

Sunday, August 1st

My gratification at receiving a letter this morning from sister Letty after a silence so long that I concluded myself no longer thought of – I do think a woman, embarazada, *has a hard time of it, sickness, heartburn, headache. I think that marriage is not what it's cracked up to be. He [Samuel] can't understand my inmost feelings. It's no fault of his but just my woman's fate. I'm half-ashamed. Many a woman with child has met greater danger and discomfort than I. This is the curse planted on Eve.*

Sooner than she anticipated, Susan's renewed vows of bravery and stoicism were put to another test. One sultry night when the shutters were ajar to catch any stray breeze that stirred, a faint vibration in the patio, a crunch of gravel startled them awake. Samuel leaped from bed, his ears straining to locate the sound, barely audible. "Put on your wrapper and slippers," he whispered to Susan, a plan of escape already forming in his mind. He stood flat against the wall by the window not daring to show himself.

Susan clutched a pillow to her chest as if to ward off an expected blow. "Do you see anything?"

"Nothing, the shade's too deep. Keep quiet."

They tensed in utter silence.

A thump, a crack above their bedroom ceiling, quick steps pattering over the flat roof. He pulled Susan behind him.

Susan's low cry of fear muffled itself against his broad shoulders. She clasped her arms more tightly around him and steadied her shaking against his solidness.

Again there was silence, again running steps that stopped right over the door to their room. Hoarse whispers, muffled exclamations. Just as a dark form swung over the low roof to drop to the ground by their door, a sentry posted at the quartermaster's house on the opposite side of the patio called out, "Who is it?" His outcry shattered the tropic stillness. A flash of lantern chased shadows from the shrubbery. "*Quien es! Parase.* Who is it? Halt!"

"Thank God in heaven," Susan prayed aloud and relaxed her tight grip on her husband's waist. "The soldiers are alerted."

They heard a wild scramble over the roof toward the back of the house, muttered *carumbas* and a snapping of tree branches. Dull thuds on packed earth told them that the intruders had landed in the horse corral. Startled whinnying echoed in the darkness.

"*Parase, ladrones,* Halt, robbers!" Many voices now took up the cry.

"They were after us, weren't they?" Susan's teeth chattered in the

August heat.

Samuel drew her to him. "Not now, not now." They clung together wordless in gratitude at yet another escape, a miraculous escape. The Magoffins crept back to bed. Samuel drifted into uneasy slumber but Susan lay thinking, phrasing and rephrasing what she would say to him in the morning. He had already promised to sell his goods to the government, but still he had delayed, hoping for a better price. Now with Jim's reported death, they couldn't delay any longer. Daylight did not weaken her resolve. Her mind was made up, she would speak out as soon as he awoke. After the terror of the past night, she knew they should take no more chances by remaining near these scenes of war.

The morning heat made Samuel roll restlessly on the rumpled covers. The shutters were still locked and the door barred. Not a breath of fresh air entered the sultry room. He reached out for Susan, but she sat up in bed, dodging his searching arms.

"We must talk over some things. We need to decide this very day, right now. It's too dangerous to remain here any longer." She drew a quivering breath.

"I know how troubled you are, dearest, but I've met the unforeseen circumstances the best I could," he began.

"You have, indeed you have. It's not for myself now that I tell you that you *must* dispose of your wagons, even at a loss, immediately. You must take me home."

"After last night, I don't blame you, Susanita, but dickering with the government takes time. I've been inquiring about a favorable trade."

"Forget profit. You have enough property in Kentucky to make us a good living."

"A man can't--" he started to say.

"Maybe a man can't forget his business, but a father can and should think more of his child than his money. Samuel, I request this sacrifice of you for our little one's sake." She paused, then added, "your brother Jim would want you to leave, if he were here to advise you."

He considered her statement. "Perhaps he would." He thought a moment. "You're right, he would. I had hoped to stay to recover his body, but that's impossible now."

"We'll honor him by naming our son James Samuel Magoffin," Susan declared, a note of pride rising in her voice. This time she didn't dodge his embrace but rested happily against him.

"All right. I'll start negotiations again this morning."

Susan tidied up their bedroom with light quick movements. She hummed aimless snatches of Kentucky songs and smiled back at her mirrored reflection, worn and sleepy-eyed as it was. Her mood of happy relief lasted for several days until a letter from Chihuahua informed them of the death of James Aull, a trader also from Missouri.

As they discussed this latest sadness, Samuel made a startling observation. "Albert Speyers in his letter noted the double coincidence of the reported death of my brother on June 23 and also the murder of James Aull in the store on June 23. It might be Aull's body, not James Magoffin's that was identified. I didn't think so then, but it could be true, it just could be that way."

Susan's heart throbbed against her ribs. "Does that mean you wish to remain to look further for Jim and not leave as you promised?"

He laid his hand over hers to assure her. "Not this time, *querida*, I might as well tell you now that the sale of our wagons is already agreed upon. Just the details of the final contract need to be guaranteed by the government. I think we'll leave for Monterrey as soon as General Cushing gathers his troops. We'll need army protection until the war is over, but the closer we get to the coast, the safer we'll be."

"You mean I should start packing?"

"Once again, dearest, and maybe for the last time."

Now she could discard their worn trail clothes, her heavy, dusty shawl and scuffed shoes, her husband's corduroy jacket, smelly and dingy from the smoke of campfires. One more last journey in the Rockaway to Monterrey, then on to Camargo where they would take a boat to New Orleans. Surely she could endure the last miles of jolting and bumping. She counted the remaining weeks of waiting when their child would be born in peace and safety at last.

A few days later Samuel brought the incredible but positive news that *James Magoffin* had been seen *alive*, that his identity had been confused with James Aull, just as speculated. Later they learned that Jim had already started home to the States, supposing that Samuel and Susan had also returned with other traders from Chihuahua.

"Isn't that just like Jim?" he asked his wife. "Not even try to contact us. Not even send a message to reassure us--"

"I wonder if he knows the hours of agonized suspense we suffered on his account?"

"Probably not, but neither do we realize what he endured during those months in that stinking cell."

Susan felt light-hearted. She joked with Comapu and Francisco, happy in the knowledge that they would have a home with the Alcalde in Camargo. She could not regret that Mrs. Hunter, her promised travel companion, had decided to wait for her husband's final discharge from the army instead of leaving earlier with Susan.

Samuel too relaxed during their last weeks of waiting. Often they sat in the patio of their rented casa. They talked over events of their journey, the dangers, the unexpected happenings, and the reported final fall of Mexico City on September 14. At last the war was over. Together they had journeyed nearly 1,300 miles, from Independence to Camargo. Susan had not only been the first American woman to travel the Santa Fe Trail, she had been the first wife of a trader to enter the hostile interior of a country at war with her homeland. "And now, *mi alma*, I'll be the first woman to return from a trading expedition to Mexico with a baby in my arms. What will Papa say about that?"

"I think, Susanita, that all his opposition to our marriage will melt away at the sight of his grandchild."

"And that will make me very happy," she whispered softly, putting away her journal for keeps.

EPILOGUE

Susan Magoffin's first diary was a handwritten account of the New York trip to purchase supplies and goods for the Santa Fe Trail. Unfortunately, this volume has long been considered lost. Her more significant Santa Fe Trail diary remained in the possession of her daughter, Jane Taylor, until 1926 when Stella Drumm, Librarian of the Missouri Historical Society, edited and annotated it for Yale Universtiy Press. This calf-skin bound notebook is still held in custody by the family heirs of Stella Drumm.

As her trail hardships increased, Susan used her diary as a means of personal expression, her doubts and fears as to the outcome of their journey. Always her love of her husband, her courage and optimism seemed to sustain her.

Though difficulties mounted, references to prayer and Bible reading showed a great reliance on God. Toward the end, Samuel too seemed less indifferent and was influenced by her belief.

A young woman today would be much franker in recording physical sensations during pregnancy. Susan mentioned them only briefly. In fact, her second pregnancy was barely alluded to (until leaving Saltillo to start for the States) -- "...my situation [does] not admit of a sea voyage for three or four months yet." A reticent attitude here was evidently caused by her knowledge that male relatives in Kentucky would read the account.

Although one senses through Susan's writing and Samuel's recorded remarks, that neither anticipated the difficulties and dangers they encountered, both exhibited unusual courage despite the temptation to turn back for home. Such was the true American pioneer spirit.

Susan Magoffin kept her diary from June 11, 1946, to September 8, 1847. Crowded among soldiers and civilians in a tiny Mexican house in Cerralvo where they awaited sailing, Susan's last entry was written with evident satisfaction. "We have said goodbye to land travel and

119

tomorrow shall take a steamboat for Camargo.''

Research done by historians in later years reveals that while still awaiting passage, Susan contracted yellow fever and was unable to travel; in late October or November, she gave birth to her second child, also a boy. The baby did not live very long. Finally, the Magoffins were able to sail from the Mexican port across the Gulf to New Orleans where they took a river boat up the Mississippi to Kentucky.

One wonders about Susan's thoughts on that last leg of her journey. It is sad she did not record her feelings on the deck of the paddle wheel steamer, watching the welcome scenery of home unfold before her. No doubt, she marveled at the fate which had taken her so far, and which, now, returned her safely to familiar surroundings. Certainly she experienced satisfaction as the first white woman to ride the Trail.

Four years later, in 1851, a third child, Jane Magoffin, was born. In 1852, the couple took their baby to Barrett's Station near Kirkwood, Missouri. Samuel gave up the Santa Fe trade to become an extensive landowner there and a prosperous real estate dealer in St. Louis County.

In 1855 Susan gave birth to another daughter, and only a few months later she herself succumbed to an untimely death. She was buried in Bellefontaine Cemetery, St. Louis.

Samuel needed a wife to help care for his two little girls. By remarkable coincidence, he married one of Susan's cousins who was named Susan Magoffin also. He lived to see his daughters grown and married, as his death did not occur until 1888 at about 88 years of age.

James, the convivial Magoffin who miraculously survived long imprisonment and trail hardship, died 20 years before Samuel, in 1868. However, after the end of the Mexican War, 1847, James continued in the Santa Fe trade and established a thriving wholesale business in a settlement called Magoffinsville, which later became part of El Paso. His son Joseph remained in El Paso and became the town's first mayor. A street is named Magoffin for the family whose descendants still lived there in 1962.

120